Even Flow

Even Flow

Darragh McManus

Winchester, UK
Washington, USA

First published by Roundfire Books, 2012
Roundfire Books is an imprint of John Hunt Publishing Ltd., Laurel House, Station Approach,
Alresford, Hants, SO24 9JH, UK
office1@o-books.net
www.o-books.com

For distributor details and how to order please visit the 'Ordering' section on our website.

Text copyright: Darragh McManus 2011

ISBN: 978 1 78099 131 3

A CIP catalogue record for this book is available from the British Library.

Design: Stuart Davies
Graphic inserts designed by Darragh McManus

Printed and bound in the USA by Edwards Brothers Malloy

We operate a distinctive and ethical publishing philosophy in all
areas of our business, from our global network of authors to
production and worldwide distribution.

CONTENTS

Copyright Acknowledgements

About the Author

Darragh McManus is a writer and journalist. His first book, *GAA Confidential*, was published by Hodder. He also published a comic novel, *Cold! Steel! Justice!!!*, as an e-book under the name Alexander O'Hara. For more than a decade he has written reviews, features and opinion columns for several papers, including The Irish Independent, The Sunday Times and The Guardian. He lives in the west of Ireland. *Even Flow* is his first crime novel. His second, *The Polka Dot Girl*, will also be published by Roundfire.

www.darraghmcmanus.com

For Majella

To avenge, in a sense, was simply to equalize, to seek a requisite balance.
Don De Lillo, *Players*

Chapter 1

Masters of the universe

HE'D never realized how cold it would be hanging upside-down outside a 32nd storey apartment.

Clifford Hudson hung there, by his ankles, hair falling away from his face, and tried to focus on this. It really was cold up that high, even though it was only September. The wind whipped about his head and bare torso, the hair on his legs pricked awake by the chill. He'd been in similar places before—climbed mountains, gone skiing, dived in deep, freezing water—but this was different. Now he had no protective clothing, no bodysuit made of cutting-edge, futuristic material, gleaming like a silver spaceman in the Alpine sun. Now he was wearing just boxer shorts, the wind was cutting into him like frozen needles, and he was *cold*. And now, of course, he was also scared.

Steve moaned again, something like, "What did I do, what did I do?" Hudson wished Steve would shut up; let him think. Let him remember how the two of them had come to be tied up, in heavy duct tape and women's clothing, strapped together like two slabs of beef in a butcher's freezer, suspended in mid-air by a rope that lead back inside the apartment window. The world spun around his head then, inverted and dizzying. Brilliant Manhattan lights, smaller pinpoints across his namesake Hudson River, the inky sea of night-time, glimpses of those black faces. The bastards were toying with them, he realized. The big one, he was spinning the rope. Playing them like a goddamn human yo-yo. Hudson could picture the other one, the talker, the one with the red bow tie, smiling as he gave his pal the order. That smug smile you could make out beneath the mask; that controlled, terrifying smile.

He felt nauseous; too much blood gone to the head, too many chemicals already in the blood. Nauseous, but still defiant. They were steadying the rope periodically, steadying him before those placards they held up to his face. Red bow tie crouched on the windowsill, leaning over toward him, whispering almost: "Everyone's watching. Go on. You'll feel better for it." He wouldn't do it. To hell with them—who did they think they were?

Hudson struggled and kicked against his binds, like a fish squirming on the hook, but it was no use. He was stuck, way up here, with Steve, who was crying like a little pussy and really starting to annoy him. Then Hudson realized that Steve had pissed down on both of them, that unmistakable hot trickle turning cold almost instantly in the night and the height. Well, this was just fucking *great*. These were Lagerfeld, pure silk, not cheap, and that idiot had spoiled them. He'd have throttled the silly little shit if he could only get his hands free.

How did this come to pass, Hudson thought? And then he remembered. Right, the party; Steve's bachelor party. Now *he* felt like crying too, crying from terror and anger but also thwarted pleasure. Fuck the three of them for ruining everything—the evening had been going so well up to that point.

It had gone just fine. Hudson was on several kinds of high by the time he arrived at Steve's apartment block in Tribeca. The stage was set, the guys had arrived; everything had been laid on for them. Steve was *in situ* from an early hour, obviously, as the guest of honor. Hudson had arranged it all: the drinks, the sounds, the little treats scattered about the apartment in broad glass bowls. Steve was his best friend, his bro, his future business partner, in all probability; and now he was getting married, and Hudson was going to make sure it was perfect. This was the least Steve deserved.

He'd popped out for an hour, to meet a few associates, once the vibe was burbling away nicely. Lively but not too crazy, not yet. You had to build up to that point, that pitch where everyone lets go. He knew all about this stuff; he was an expert in helping others to have a good time. Call it a God-given talent. Now Hudson reached forward and pressed the intercom for Steve's apartment. A voice answered, slightly drunk: "Come on up." He tried to place it as the door snapped open and he moved inside. Might be that jack-off Leopold, though Hudson couldn't remember inviting him. Leopold—what a stupid name. He'd have to be a jack-off with a name like that.

Hudson moved up several flights of stairs, their bare concrete walls and metal steps, the designer communist sort of look that was so hip with certain types of people in certain areas. Passing the smooth steel doors of the elevator on each floor, and passing them by: he took pride in his physical fitness. More than 30 stories was nothing, coked up or not; in fact, he considered it a challenge, to complete this trek while under the influence of something or other. Steve was softer, lazier; he was prone to weight gain and the easy option. He'd go to fat within a few years, like both their fathers. But Hudson wouldn't let that happen to him.

He passed a young woman on the stairs, about two-thirds of the way up. She was very good-looking, showing a lot of thigh and a hint of tit. She eyed him nervously as they approached one another, leaning against the wall to allow him by. Hudson snapped on his sharpest killer smile and lifted a hand: "'S'okay. Don't be nervous, baby. I'm going to a party." She stood there, looking down at the ground, as he continued upward, and then his cell phone rang. He pulled it out, tiny and beetle-black, flipping open the receiver.

"Wassup? Yeah, it's me. I'm on my way... I'm on the stairs, fucko. I'm right outside your... Yeah, I got it... I *got* it. I told you I got it, you dick... Ha ha ha ha! Yeah, you do that, man. You keep them on the boil for me... Yeah, see ya in a second."

Hudson kept climbing until he reached a massive, dark wood double-door, pressing the buzzer. The door swung open and he stepped through into an absolutely gorgeous apartment. Man, Steve sure knew how to decorate; or, at least, Christine did. Groovy, mellow dance music slinked from strategically located speakers as he walked into the room, surveying the scene.

The boys were all in town—young, lean, confident, in sharp suits and studiously unremarkable haircuts. They went to the kind of barbers who charge 500 bucks to make you look as if you haven't just been to the barbers. The drink was flowing down and the talk getting louder by the sentence. Men stood around or lounged on pale-colored couches, knocking back beers and picking at plates of nuts and discussing business and sports and how close they were to fucking that hot little blonde in marketing. Nobody smoked, oddly. Hudson passed a table over which two of his friends leaned, fingers pressed to their noses and an almost absurd air of concentration about them. He dipped a finger into the bowl beside them and sucked on it— *zing*—that's good stuff. No cheap shit for Steve on his special night. Across the room two others were actually wrestling; real infantile crap. One of them jostled a vase Hudson had bought Steve for his birthday. He made a mental note to self: throw these assholes out within the hour.

At the far side of the room, on a lower level, a group huddled together, looking at something. Hudson smiled—everything was set to perfection—and caught his reflection in a long mirror. His black, clipped hair, dark eyes, hard-earned physique under a suit that couldn't have fit better if it was his own skin. He smiled and nodded to himself. He felt satisfied. Then Steve sprang toward him, seemingly from nowhere. He had always been quieter, smaller, a paler presence; people didn't tend to notice him too often next to Hudson.

Steve yelled, arms outstretched, "*Heeeyy*!! Hud, you faggot! You're back!"

They clasped hands and Hudson said, "Steve. The pleasure, as always, is yours."

"Did you bring it? You brought it, right? *Tell* me you brought it…"

Hudson patted his inside pocket. "Relax, man. I got it right here. Shit. I *got* it, bro."

Steve reached forward and Hudson slapped his hand away, saying, "Ah-ah-*ah*. All in good time, my man. All in good time. A little alcohol and light entertainment first."

Outside, three figures in tuxedos moved through the black, shining night. Each had a small rucksack on his back. One of them was huge, six foot five, powerful across the chest. One was slim, light-footed, a little shorter than average. The one in the center was lean and reasonably tall. His dark-red dickey-bow, in contrast to the others' black ties, was vivid against the whiteness of his shirt. It looked like blood on virgin snow.

Hudson strode through the room, grabbing a drink off a table as he walked to the lower level, Steve in tow. The group parted to make way for him—it felt natural, respectful, this movement aside—and revealed two women sitting and embracing on a thick rug as the crowd egged them on. One had her face buried in the crook of the other's neck. They stroked each other's upper arms and hips, languidly, detached somehow. The women stopped then and looked up, eyes flitting from face to face. They were young—one very young—and pretty, dressed in cheap fabrics and gaudy colors. Tight pants, crop tops, large hoop earrings swinging against loosened strands of hair. They looked around uneasily. They looked at Hudson.

He examined them for a moment, nodded and said, "Mm-hm. Not bad. Not bad at all. They'll do," then turned back to the group and lifted his drink to eye level.

"Okay, men. Raise a glass and call a toast for our good friend Steve Ainsworth, who has decided to finally make an honest woman out of Christine. How she puts up with the prick I dunno, but I guess all those blow-jobs she's been fortunate enough to give *me* have helped her through it some ways."

Hudson smiled. The crowd laughed, none more than Steve, who shook his head like an indulgent parent. Hud was the funniest son of a bitch he'd ever known.

"Anyway, anyway, Steve, you're our main guy and I'm proud to be your best man. I'm sure you and Christine will be very happy together, and whatever you need, you know you only gotta ask."

Steve nodded his appreciation.

"So fellas, raise your glass for a great fucking guy and a great lady: to Steve and Christine."

A chorus of "Steve and Christine."

Hudson said, "Stevie boy, this is your last night of freedom, so enjoy it well. We got booze, we got coke, we got every fucking thing you could ask for. And, of course..." He pointed behind him at the two women. "...we got, uh..." He turned, stared at them, shrugged. "Well. Whatever their names are. They're here to please *you*, Steve, so what's it gonna be?"

Steve wiped his hand across his mouth, wiped a smile onto his face as two friends slid a chair under his behind. He settled in, his glassy eyes brightening, staring at the two girls.

"I wanna watch, Hud. I wanna watch 'em."

Hudson nodded. He took a swig from his drink and said, "You heard the man, ladies. Do what you're good for."

Now *this* is the moment: here is where the pitch is reached. Someone dimmed the lights, someone else struck up a spot over that corner of the room; Hudson had all the angles covered. He felt a thrill, an electric jolt, spiral up and down his spine as the girls got into it. The crowd moved in around them, pressing, urging, as the two women pulled each other's clothes off. Their hair mussed up around those pretty faces, asses in the air, panties strewn like rubble around their ankles. The older one fell over, legs splayed and surprise in her expression, and a cheer rose. Hudson slipped a pill into his mouth and let the moment take him over.

He saw everything; he saw them do everything, every fucking thing they were ordered. It became like a film reel then, black-

7

and-white but ultra-defined. No, not a film reel—a photographic slide-show. Image after image after image, metered out, steady, vivid, under his control. The women pressing their tongues into each other's mouths. Plastic toys clutched, or discarded on the shag carpet. Obscure, hardly definable body parts: someone's shoulder or thigh, a scrap of pubic hair, the Sahara ripple of skin over rib cage. The tatty fabrics of their whore outfits. Male hands entering the picture, to guide them, force them together, or clenched in a fist of exultation. The boys whooped and hollered, patting Steve on the back as he sat there, pleased and horny. They encouraged the women to do more, go further, be wilder. Manic expressions on the watching crowd: sex- and booze- and drug-crazed. Grinding teeth, sweat stains on their shirts; nods of validation and camaraderie. The spotlight pure and unflinching, the murky bass on the music echoing throughout the apartment—that subterranean, relentless beat…

Eventually Hudson stepped in and pulled the girls apart. They cowered, scuttling backward, covering their nakedness with their hands. They looked disheveled and beaten-down; their make-up had streaked on their faces.

Hudson said, "Alrighty. Well, I think we all enjoyed that a *whole* lot. I know you did, anyway, Stevie boy."

Everyone laughed, including Steve. A guy in a black polo shirt and square glasses said, "He was moaning like a bitch!"

More laughter. Hudson raised a hand. "Alright, alright. That's enough of that. We're here to party with Steve, fellas, not to degrade him; 'cause after all…" He looked down at the two women. "…that's what *you're* here for."

The three men in tuxedos were approaching the apartment building. Ten yards from the main door they pulled black balaclavas over their heads and leather gloves onto their hands. The figure in the red bow tie held his finger poised over the buzzer. He spoke in a deep, quiet, slightly distorted voice without turning back.

"Are you ready for this? Both of you?"

The big one flicked away the end of a cigarette. The small one breathed out loudly through pursed lips. They both nodded and hummed affirmation.

"Okay, then. Onward we go."

He pressed the buzzer; no voice answered but the door opened. They entered the building.

Hudson reached into his jacket and pulled out a dead mouse, half-wrapped in tissue. It sat in his hand, limp and disgusting, though he didn't appear bothered by it. The group started jostling, leaning on one another's shoulders, monkey noises, a charge of excitement.

"Oh, *shit*! Oh, baby! You cannot be serious!"

"This is gonna be so fucking *cool*!"

Hudson looked at them, a solemn, almost teacherly expression: "I can't be serious? I'm always serious." He turned to the two women. "Ladies, I'd like you to meet a good friend of mine—Spanky the mouse—sadly, recently deceased."

He held the animal down to their faces. They turned away in revulsion, eyes down, hands to their mouths. The younger one rubbed her nose, sniffling.

"Well, come on," Hudson said. "Don't be rude. Say hello to Spanky. You're gonna be getting a hell of a lot closer to our little pal here, so it's good that you get to know each other a little better first."

Steve sat up in his chair, gleaming, gazing at his friend. He said, "Aw, you are the *bomb*, Hud. You are the fucking bomb. You are *it*, man."

Hudson smiled. "Anything for a friend, Stevie boy. Now, girls—you know what to do with little Spanky here."

The younger girl clutched her friend's shoulder and mumbled, "I don't think... I don't wanna do this..."

The older one drew some fortitude, then, from somewhere. She sat straighter and looked at Hudson directly, her breasts bare, her teeth set, a pulse in the graceful length of her neck.

She said, "Hey, she doesn't feel too good. My friend is feeling kinda sick, okay? I think we should call it a night here. You can...you know, you can keep some of the money..."

Hudson leaned in close, his lips almost brushing her ear. "Uh-uh. I don't think we're gonna call it a night. I think you're gonna do what you've been fucking paid to do. What we *tell* you to do." He stood and addressed the assembled masses. "Right, guys?"

A great cheer; then, as if by some spontaneous instinct of the collective, they began to chant, unprompted: "Fuck the mouse...fuck the mouse..." The two women glanced at each other apprehensively. The younger one shook her head, her gaze half-focused on the fuzzy middle-distance. Hudson threw the dead animal onto the rug and glared at them. The chant continued, louder, more playful but also more insistent, the pitch building again. The girls didn't move. Hudson set his jaw and breathed rapidly through his nose; he was not a patient man.

"Fuck the mouse...fuck the mouse..."

Another 20 or 30 seconds, and he'd had enough of this shit. The money had been paid, time for the action. Hudson leaned forward to grab one of them by the hair, either one, to force the little cunt's face down to the ground, when one side of the apartment door crashed open. It blew inward, the heavy wood lifting at the bottom, splinters like confetti shooting into the air, and hung unsteadily by its upper hinge. The room felt silent, though the music continued to play; a communal holding of breath, as everyone froze in their tracks, waiting to see what was coming next. Even Hudson didn't act.

The three men in tuxedoes walked into the apartment, flicking the main light switch on entering. The place flooded with the soft yellow glow of roof spotlights. Two stood with their hands behind their backs; the one in the red bow tie stepped forward, raised a finger to his chin and said, "'Fuck the mouse, fuck the mouse...' Hmm. Fuck a *mouse*? What kinda... Did you ever hear anything like that before, Waters?"

The smaller man replied, "Nah. Sounds pretty strange to me, Wilde."

The one calling himself Wilde said, "What 'bout you, Whitman?"

The big man shrugged lazily. "Uh-uh. Never heard of that. You?"

Wilde shook his head. "Can't say I have. But I don't get out much these days, so, you know..."

Hudson acted then, his pride clicking back on like the light switch. He strode toward them, to the front of the crowd, incandescent with rage.

"What...? Who the *fuck* do you think you are, coming in here like this!? This is a private party! What is this? Some kind of fucking *joke*?"

Wilde emitted a short laugh, slightly muffled by his mask.

Hudson spluttered, "So this *is* a joke, right? Some son of a bitch put you up to this. *Right*!?"

Wilde said, "No. I realize you can't tell with these balaclavas, but we're not joking. Show him how serious we are, Whitman."

Whitman and Waters brought their hands around the front — each held a gun with a silencer. Whitman looked to Wilde.

"Who?"

"Anyone."

Whitman stepped forward and shot one guy at random, through the foot. He dropped to the ground, screaming in pain, an almost comical look of surprise on his face. Everyone gasped in shock but didn't move, didn't panic. There was a weird air of sedation — paralysis by fear, maybe. Hudson stood there, stunned momentarily, then that cocky belligerence reasserted itself once more.

He yelled, "Wha-? You mother*fucker*!!" and rushed toward

Wilde. But Whitman moved too fast: he was between them, pressing the gun against Hudson's cheek. The barrel pushed into his skin, creating a pallid ellipse.

Wilde sighed, almost inaudibly, and said, "Don't. Don't move, don't try to knock his hand away, and don't speak another fucking word. We hadn't planned to kill anyone tonight, but we're, ah...*flexible*. Whitman here already has a thing about yuppies, so don't tempt him. Now..." He looked around the assembled company. "...which one of you is Steven Ainsworth?"

No response for a moment; then Steve meekly showed himself, shuffling through the mass of men, a terrified expression, glancing from left to right as if seeking encouragement.

He said, "What...what is this? Is this a robbery? Do you want...? Here." Steve took off his watch. It was a beautiful model: Swiss, virtually nuclear precision in the timekeeping. "Take this. I've got money. And they've got money. Come on, guys. Give him your money. Give him your fucking money!"

Wilde strolled past Hudson and Whitman, locked in their glacial embrace, and said, "Keep it. We don't want money. We came here to make a statement, nothing more."

Steve remained where he was, his watch proffered before him like the alms of a penitent. He looked baffled, and cold somehow, crouched in that ridiculous position; he dared not look to the side as Waters moved past him, flanking Wilde, covering him, waving his gun to clear the crowd. Whitman threw Hudson aside and moved back to cover the door. Hudson took a few steps back, away from the centre, skulking, nursing his bruises.

Wilde bent down to the two women, who flinched slightly. They were very pretty. One was darker, with shortish hair, a strong jaw-line, a plump lower lip and a flash of intelligence in her eyes; the other, the younger one, was fair, pale even, with long hair in a ponytail which had gotten skewed to the side, a slight overbite, ice-gray eyes, and delicate, long lashes. Wilde smiled, in a way he hoped would be reassuring; he realized the peculiarity of his garb. He reached out a hand, slowly.

The older girl recoiled and said, "Don't...! Please. Don't...don't hurt us. Don't hurt her."

Wilde withdrew his hand, saying gently to her, "I won't hurt you. Get dressed."

She looked at him, unsure.

"Go on," he said. "It's okay. Get dressed."

The older girl began scrabbling around for her clothes, sorting through the scattered detritus of the last half-hour. Wilde reached behind for a brightly colored woolen throw and wrapped it around the younger woman, embracing her shoulders. She was shaking.

He whispered, "Hey. It's okay. Don't be frightened. We're not going to hurt you. Look at me. Look at my eyes."

Her eyes remained fixed on the floor.

"It's alright, sweetheart. Are you looking at me? Don't be frightened. What's your name?"

The girl looked up then, her gaze at some point on his forehead. She said, "It's...Dorothy. My name is Dorothy."

"Dorothy. Okay. What a pretty name. How old are you, Dorothy?"

A tall, extremely skinny man in an ironically garish shirt and yellow suspenders bounded forward, waving his arms around. He said, "Hey, what the fuck, man? Just let us go, alright? If you wanna do whatever you wanna do with the hookers, man, that's o..."

Waters smacked him in the nose with the butt of the gun, that horrible bone squelch. He crumpled in a heap, blood pouring through his fingers, legs kicking like an upended insect.

"Anyone else feel like they have a contribution to make? Please, feel free," Waters said.

Wilde turned back to Dorothy. "It's alright, now. Hey. Are you looking at me?"

She started to cry. Dry sobs at first, her shoulders shaking, and then the tears rolled down her pale cheeks. The other woman, now dressed, scootched across on her backside to console her friend.

Dorothy said, "I'm...17. I don't know how... I didn't mean to end up doing this. I'm not, um... Amy just asked me to come along..."

Wilde said, "Okay. It's alright, sweetheart. Get dressed." He turned to Amy. "Do you have money?"

She nodded yes. Wilde stood up, looked around, pointed to a heavyset guy in shiny trousers.

"You. Take off your watch, all your jewelry, and give me your wallet. Now."

The man did as he was ordered. Wilde held it out to Amy, saying, "Here. Might as well get something, right? Take it."

Amy took it, holding it gingerly, away from her.

"Help her get dressed and...can you hail a taxi?" Wilde asked.

"Yeah... Hey—thanks."

Wilde nodded, "Sure", and turned to the group of men. "Now—Steven Ainsworth. Come here, Steven."

Steve hesitated, swallowing heavily, forestalling events. Then a realization: there is no slithering out of this. He could practically feel the heavy hands of his relieved friends on his back as he walked toward Wilde, slowly and nervously. He looked around for support again; his friends looked away.

He said, "Hey, look. I'm not sure... What's going on here, dude? What are you doing in my place?"

Wilde ignored him and moved to the window, the large window with that coveted view of the river by night. It looked like the backdrop to a late-night chat-show: the twinkling lights, the miniature squares of neon, the blue-black mirror of the Hudson. Almost too beautiful.

"Steven Ainsworth," he said. "Steve to his friends. Futures trader with a blue-chip company. Father an investment banker, mother a lady of leisure. Membership of a country club, a gentleman's club, an expensive health and racquet club…all the trappings of a gilded life."

He paused, one gloved finger to his chin. Steve moved to speak and Wilde raised the finger, cutting him off, like a hammy detective explaining the murder.

"Engaged to Christine De Beers; Chris to *her* friends. Ceremony in two days' time in a small, beautifully kept uptown church. Guests include several big wheels in finance, industry, the judiciary, and at least one high-profile politician who, if rumor is to be believed, would have fit in quite well at this cozy little *soirée*."

He turned back to Steve. "Uh-huh. I know *all* about you, Steven."

Steve lost his cool, finally: stress and irritation getting the upper hand on terror. He said, "Look, what *is* this, you shithead? Whaddyou *want*!?"

Wilde nodded at Waters who slapped Steve, with his hand, on the side of the head, not too hard.

"Shut your mouth and open your ears. We're getting to the good part soon." Wilde returned to that gorgeous, heartbreaking view. "So Steve and all his friends decide to have a little party; something to mark the occasion, as it were. A select group invited round to these elegant surroundings; a few drinks, a little coke, a lot of bullshit, a couple of beautiful girls…what could be finer?"

Waters shrugged and said, "I can't think of anything, Wilde."

"But you had to go overboard, Steven. You weren't satisfied with that. None of you. You weren't satisfied with taking the drugs and talking the bullshit; you weren't even satisfied with having sex with the beautiful girls."

The women had dressed without anybody really noticing it. They looked different now, even in the same clothes: more grave, more inflexible, but also less tethered to now. It seemed like a part of Amy and Dorothy had come loose and floated away. They stood behind Wilde, who gestured to them.

"Look at them! They're *gorgeous*. What guy wouldn't want to be with a woman who looks like that, even if he is paying for it? Hey, I'm a man—I understand these things."

He nodded at the two women, and they moved to leave. The crowd parted for them. Dorothy looked at her feet; Amy stared at each man, straight on, with contempt.

Wilde continued, "But that wasn't enough for you pricks. You had to go a little further. You're so fucking tired and cynical; you've had so many good things for so long, so much sex and money and power, that you're incapable of feeling real pleasure or joy anymore. You've become empty inside and need to degrade others to fill that hole." He leaned forward. "Am I correct, Steven?"

Steve flushed, waved his hands. "Hey, wait. Look, okay? We didn't... They're okay. We didn't hurt them, alright? We... How the fuck did you know about this, anyway?"

"How did we know? We hear things, Steven. Our reach is long and our friends are everywhere... The truth is we didn't know. We picked you at random. We found out who had hired girls for a party tonight, and we picked you." Wilde rested his arms on the windowsill, gazed out the window. "But it doesn't matter, 'cause you're all the same. Could be you, could be some other asshole across town. You're a *type*, Steven: you're a particular kind of guy with particular tastes. We didn't even know what shit you'd pull tonight, but we knew what shit you'd pull tonight, you understand me? And you'll do fine. You'll make the same statement as anyone else."

Steve pointed behind him, fright in his eyes, saying, "It wasn't me, okay? It was Hud. Hud arranged the whole thing. I just... Hud brought them here. I just asked for some hookers for my bachelor party and he..."

Wilde said, "So you're passing the blame to your friend

there?"

Waters laughed, sardonic. "Ah! No honor among thieves anymore, Wilde."

Hudson took a step forward, squaring himself. He was over that hump of indignity; now he was angry with these cocksuckers.

"Steve, shut your stupid, whiny fucking mouth or I will shut it for you." He pointed at Wilde. "And fuck you, okay, pal? Fuck...*you*!! They're *whores*, you asshole! What did they expect coming here? Tea and fucking *cake*!? Look at them! They're just whores!"

Amy and Dorothy had reached the door. Amy walked back toward Hudson and spat in his face, then turned and left. Hudson fumed, itching to react, to slap her down, to show everyone who was the boss of this situation.

Whitman bowed to the two women as they left, an extravagant stoop, and said, "'Night, ladies. Take care, now."

Wilde stepped forward and addressed the rest of the crowd: "All the rest of you: get out of here. Take your jackets and get the fuck out. Go straight home. Don't try to catch up with Amy and Dorothy there—we'll be watching."

The men began gathering their things, sheepishly, awkwardly, furtive glances at the three men with the three guns. And at the two who would remain. Wilde turned to Steve.

"Steven and his belligerent pal—you're staying here. We have big plans for the two of you."

Hudson shouted, "Hey, look, you sick bastard. I've got friends, okay? I know people. You don't wanna fuck with me..."

Waters laughed again. "Oh, yeah—we've seen how *your* friends act, 'Hud.'"

"We don't want to fuck with you?" Wilde asked. "Oh, but we *do*, Hud. A sweet-looking boy like you? We want to fuck with you *very* much. Whitman—the door."

The last partygoer exited, a dissipated shadow stealing away.

The door still hung from the hinge. Whitman pushed hard and quick, jamming it into the frame. The wood made a squeak of resistance to set the teeth on edge. He remained there, bulky and soundless, gun resting on one huge bicep. Waters and Wilde faced Steve and Hudson, who had instinctually moved closely together, back to back, their hands out in front, a motion of warding away. Strength in numbers, but now there were only two. For the first time Hudson could feel his spirit, his intrinsic courage, begin to leak away. He looked at the masked men and felt small.

"Big plans, Hud. Big plans and big statements, and you're the first," Wilde said. "But consider yourself fortunate: people will remember you for a long time because of this. You *and* your friend."

Delete   **Reply** ▼   **Forward** ▼   **Move...** ▼

Date: Wed, 15 Oct 2007 17:52:39

From: "Fingal O'Flahertie" <wildeimaginings@hotmail.com>

Subject: Tuesday's Musique Non Stop column

To: groganmuso@yahoo.com

Dear Ms. Grogan,
Regarding your piece on Christina Aguilera's forthcoming live DVD: was it
really necessary to describe the singer as – and here I quote – a 'slut', a
'tramp', a 'slut' again and, my favorite, 'a music biz version of every small
town's guaranteed easy lay'? I mean, what's with the abuse here? What's with
the woman-hating language? Correct me if I'm wrong, but you *are* a woman.
Yours, a puzzled reader.
PS. Personally, I can't abide either Christina Aguilera or her music, but that's
beside the point.

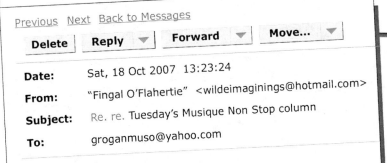

Delete   **Reply** ▼   **Forward** ▼   **Move...** ▼

Date: Sat, 18 Oct 2007 13:23:24

From: "Fingal O'Flahertie" <wildeimaginings@hotmail.com>

Subject: Re. re. Tuesday's Musique Non Stop column

To: groganmuso@yahoo.com

Dear Ms. Grogan,
Thanks for your reply. I do understand that yours is, as you say, a
'provocative' opinion column, and I never mentioned anything about
restricting your freedom of speech. I'm just curious, that's all. Curious as
to why a woman would use such language about another woman. And
would you use the same terminology to describe, say, a male rock star
who screwed around at every possible opportunity? Would you call Elton
John a 'mincing little faggot', or whatever? Or have you even thought
about this inconsistency?
Yours, still puzzled.
PS. By the way, in response to your description of me as a 'typical uptight
moaning feminist anachronism, giving other women a bad name': I'm
male. Duh.

Previous Next Back to Messages

| Delete | Reply ▼ | Forward ▼ | Move... ▼ |

This message is not flagged. [Flag message - Mark as Unread]

Date: Sun, 19 Oct 2007 20:58:16

From: "Fingal O'Flahertie" <wildeimaginings@hotmail.com>

Subject: Re. re. re. re. Tuesday's Musique Non Stop column

To: groganmuso@yahoo.com

Dear Ms. Grogan,
What a charming response. I'm amazed my ISP swear-checker actually let that through.
Anyway: do you know what an 'Uncle Tom' is? Can you spell 'sell-out'?
Yours in disgust (and yeah, still puzzled).

Chapter 2

Karma TV

JONATHON Bailey was widely known as a pompous ass, which was not something he would necessarily deny. News anchors should have a certain gravitas, he had always felt, a fixedness, an oak-like sturdiness. Viewers didn't want someone they could "relate to", someone like them passing on random information. They wanted—they *needed*—an authoritative figure, who would inform, console, and reassure. Someone who knew more than them. If others chose to misread that as self-importance, that was their problem.

He also looked the part, from lacquered hair to beautifully tailored Italian suit—tanned, late middle-age, a little jowly, a sort of Robert Redford cragginess settling into his face. Bailey fixed the cameras in the Network 4 news studio with the unruffled gaze typical of his species and intoned, in a carefully modulated timbre of voice, "...and the vote is expected to go *against* the motion to rezone that area. This could spell disaster for Imprimatur, the consortium of developers behind the project. In other financial news..."

Watching from the sidelines were Cathy Morrissey, production manager for the network's news output, and her research assistant, Patrick Broder. They both rested their weight on one leg, hips cocked slightly out and up, and shook their heads, almost to the same meter, in sardonic dismissal of their charge.

"Jesus. Jonathon's got that constipated expression again," Cathy said. "I hate when he gets that. It scares the old folks watching. Makes 'em change the channel."

"He looks in pain. I wonder if he's alright? Genuinely."

"He always gets like that when his wife kicks him out. She caught him cheating. Again."

Cathy was in her late thirties, with thick, chestnut brown hair and a palpable quickness to her aspect, a sparky smartness. She was short and pear-shaped, though not unattractively propor-tioned. She wore chic, dark green glasses and a communications headset, its thin black tongue snaking around to her mouth from somewhere within that mass of hair. Patrick was tall and rangy, in his mid-twenties with fair, cropped hair. He was a handsome young man, though perhaps a little fine-featured for some, with his long, slim nose, pale-blue eyes, and unusually slender neck; the sort of look that tends to get labeled "pretty", whether as a compliment or insult or both.

He hoisted the clipboard in his hands and said, "No way."

Cathy nodded, her abundant waves of hair bobbing gently with the movement. "Uh-huh. He was getting friendly with one of her girlfriends. Mrs. Jonathon caught 'em doing it on the kitchen table, I heard."

"Get outta here. You heard. You heard where?"

"I heard, okay? Hey, if nothing else it should give them something to talk about at coffee mornings. Aw...here he comes..."

She stiffened, an infinitesimal motion of readiness, as Bailey completed his spiel: "...and Oliver Rusnak will be here with the market prices after these commercials", then shifted his well-tailored bulk from behind the desk and walked to where Cathy and Patrick stood. Bailey dabbed at his forehead with a tissue, and when he spoke it was in his own, mildly abrasive accent, pure Bronx. This interchange of news-casting voice and real voice never failed to amuse Cathy. And it also made him seem more human and less potent, less the god almighty asshole he pretended to be. It helped her do her job, which partly constituted keeping Bailey happy. She knew how to play him, how to calm him down or massage his colossal ego; sometimes, she even felt strangely fond of him, but quickly dismissed this as irrationality.

"Jesus Christ, Cathy. I told you I wanted the rezoning piece *before* the item on water tax," Bailey said. "You think people wanna hear about water tax at this hour of the morning? We need to catch them first, *then* hold them. Goddamn water tax."

Cathy said, in her customized pacifying voice, "Sorry, Jonathon. I just thought..."

"And could you turn down the goddamn heating in here, please? I'm baking to death under those lights as it is."

"Sure, Jonathon. I'll see to it."

Bailey turned to Patrick, as if he'd just seen him. "And who the hell are you?"

"This is Patrick Broder," Cathy said. "He hasn't been with us long."

"I asked him. And what do you do around here, Patrick Broder?"

Patrick said, "I'm, uh, I'm in research, Mr. Bailey. I'm a researcher in the news department."

Bailey handed him a coffee cup, off-white with a section of Van Gogh's Sunflowers printed on the side.

"No, you're not. Right now you're the guy who's gonna bring me some coffee. Cafeteria down the hall to your right. Black, two sugars. Ask Margaret behind the counter. She knows what I like. Thanks, kid."

Patrick smiled, a little embarrassed, and left with the cup and a bemused expression. Bailey winced in discomfort.

"Jesus, my... Uuh. My goddamn ulcer," he said. "I had it, then it left, and now it's back worse than ever. Do you know how painful an ulcer is?"

"Um, no, but my mother once..."

Bailey ignored her and leaned in conspiratorially.

"Listen, uh, Cathy. There's something... I need to ask you a favor, but it's a little...sensitive."

He smiled, a horrible shark-tooth rictus really, and nodded rapidly. Cathy pretended not to know what he was talking about, frowning in mock concentration; this also amused her greatly.

Bailey continued, "Okay. Um...thing is, Cathy, as you've probably heard on the, uh, grapevine around this place... 'Cause I know how rumors spread. I know how people hear things, and then someone else hears something different, and the whole thing just snowballs... Hell, I *invented* some of those rumors..."

One of the floor staff approached. "There's a package at reception for you to sign, Mr. Bailey."

"Yeah, I'll be right..." Bailey said. "Okay, Cathy. The thing is... I need somewhere to, to, to *stay* for a little while. 'Cause Karen and me, we're, uh, we're having a few difficulties and, uh..."

"Oh, I'm so sorry, Jonathon. I hadn't heard."

"Yeah, well... She's kicked me out, and it's for good this time. I need somewhere to stay, to live, and I'm an old man, Cathy, I haven't rented an apartment in 35 years and..."

Cathy smiled indulgently. "And you'd like me to help you find somewhere."

Bailey nodded and said, "Yes. Yes, I need your help. I need... But you gotta keep this quiet, okay? You know what this business is like—one crack in the goddamn happy family façade and suddenly you're not so suitable as the respectable face of broadcasting, you know what I mean? That's why I'm asking *you*. 'Cause I know I can rely on your, ah...discretion."

"No problem. Leave it with me. I'll..." She stopped, her eyes up toward some point above their heads, listening as a message came through on her earpiece. "Uh-huh. Okay. Be there in a second." Cathy looked back at Bailey. "Go get your package, Jonathon. And listen, don't worry. I'll take care of it."

Patrick had returned. "There you go, Mr. Bailey. Black, two sugars. And Margaret says to say hi."

"Thanks, Paul. And thank *you*, Cathy."

Cathy nodded, saying, "Sure."

Bailey left, clutching his cup, wiping sweat from his face, his leathery cheeks. Cathy shook her head. She looked tired suddenly.

"What was all that about?" Patrick said. "I didn't think the old fart knew the words 'thank you.' He couldn't get my name right for starters."

"Oh, don't mind Jonathon. He's brusque and arrogant, but somewhere underneath that plastic hair and deep tan there's a decent human being."

Patrick raised an arch eyebrow. "Really?"

"Well, half-human anyway. Okay—duty calls."

For such a big concern, the Network 4 reception was surprisingly small. A double outer door, leading in from a small, canopied front area; a gray tiled floor, with a winding stair straight ahead, a large reception desk to the right, and a corridor beyond that leading to elevators and various administration offices. There was also a door to the left, just inside the front entrance, and it occurred to Bailey, as he approached the desk, that he'd never known what lay behind it. He shrugged and let the thought pass—he didn't care, one way or another. The receptionist, a baby-faced woman of about 30 in too much make-up, was on a telephone call. It sounded personal. Bailey leaned in toward the counter.

"Hi, uuh..." He clocked her nametag. "Jennifer. There's a package here? For me?"

He drew the outline of a rectangle in the air with his fingers. Jennifer smiled sweetly and pointed to a courier standing by the door, clutching a plain package and a clipboard.

Bailey scowled and said, "*Thank* you."

The courier was very tall and well-built, dressed in motorcycle leathers and still wearing his helmet. Bailey could see his own warped reflection in it as he approached. He didn't like the view—it made his face look fat. He pointed back behind the man's head, to the entrance doors, saying, "Didn't you read the sign outside? 'All couriers must remove helmets on entering building'—something like that. You're still wearing yours."

The courier flipped up the visor halfway. Only the lower part of his face was properly visible. He had a discolored tooth on the bottom row and dark stubble across the jaw-line; the sort of man who'd have to shave more than once a day if he worked somewhere like here.

He sighed and said, "Just sign for it, sir, please. I'm on a tight schedule today, you know?"

Bailey grumbled to himself and signed the clapboard. The courier handed him the package, saying, "Feels like a videotape. Enjoy watching it, sir."

He turned to leave. Bailey raised a hand after him.

"Hey, hold on there. I'm not sure I like your goddamned attitude. Hold it, mister. I wanna know what company you work for…"

The courier ignored him and walked out the door.

Bailey muttered, "Goddamn disrespectful punk." He wondered if the dizzy girl on reception had witnessed any of that. A sly glance to his left assured him she hadn't.

Cathy and Patrick stood outside, leaning against a heavy door, sipping coffees from spongy polystyrene cups, eyes closed, each easing the kinks out of their neck. A pre-recorded insert was going out at that moment; 15 minutes of a break for an overworked floor staff. She lit a cigarette, thanking Christ for the invention of both nicotine and pre-recorded inserts, and offered Patrick the pack.

"You wanna smoke? Oh, no, I remember. You don't. You're a regular clean-livin' guy, huh, Patrick?"

Patrick laughed and said, "I'm a monk, baby. Pure of heart and pure of deed. Nah, I cut it up a little from time to time. I mean, I drink beer, you know, I've been known to enjoy the odd joint or two… Just never gotten the taste for tobacco, I guess."

"You drink beer. Well, that'll do for now; we can get you hooked on these things further down the line. Hey, why don't we grab a few tonight? I'm meeting my husband later on. Have you met Philip? We'll be in Doyle's around eight. You know it? The

Irish pub there on Thirtieth? Near Penn Station."

"Yeah, I've passed by a few times, I know where it is. Sure, why not? Doyle's at eight. Sounds good."

Cathy smiled up at him, squinting into the sunshine behind his head. "Well, okay then."

One of the floor staff opened the door, glanced from side to side and spotted them where they stood. Relief and agitation fought for control of his face as he leaned toward them, out of breath.

"Cathy, you... You gotta see this. It's Jonathon, he's got something... This is some strange shit, Cathy. He got a videotape delivered ten minutes ago, and it's... You gotta come see this."

Cathy and Patrick look at each other, mystified. He smiled wryly and said, "Not DVD? How retro."

She said, "Now what the hell's this all about?"

He shrugged and held out his hand, directing her toward the door.

"Let's find out. After you."

Despite the notorious ban on smoking in all public buildings, introduced to New York some years previously, the small screening room was blue with smoke by the time they entered. Cathy smelled it immediately: these were Bailey's cigars, bloated, disgusting things whose reek hung around for days afterward. (Not too dissimilar to their owner, she joked.) Nobody seemed to mind, strangely; in fact, nobody really seemed to notice at all. Bailey, Cathy presumed, thought of himself as too important a figure to the corporation to worry about a smack on the fingers for breaking the law; besides, he was rich enough to pay the fine without too much anguish. He sat around a console, with George Oliver, the station technical supervisor, and two or three of the floor staff, watching video footage with amazed expressions.

Cathy took a few steps into the room and said, "Jonathon— you've got something for me to see."

Bailey whirled around, eyes and mouth wide open, and pointed back to the screen. For the first time since Cathy had known him, this consummate broadcasting professional genuinely appeared to be dumbfounded.

"This is... I've been in this business for almost four decades and I've never seen something like this. It's unbelievable."

"What is it? What's unbelievable?"

Bailey gestured to one of the staffers, his waving arm dragging contrails of soot-gray smoke though the glow of the screen. "Rewind the tape. Come on, come on, rewind the tape. Come up here, Cathy."

Cathy and Patrick moved forward as the video started to play again. It looked, on first glance, to be a fairly professional production—while the camera was handheld, with jerky movements, the cutting was clean and the background music smoothly inserted. Credits zoomed forward in a cartoonish typeface, fat and bright yellow: "Karma TV. A 3W Production." Then a man's face appeared on screen—dark hair, flushed complexion. He looked scared, and his hair seemed to be pulling upward from his head. Something odd about this picture.

A voice was heard from off-screen: "'The sordid confessions of a real man's man': take one." Something odd about the voice, too: mechanized, set to an unusual vibration; inauthentic somehow.

Then the man on screen starting talking, his eyes flitting from the camera to a point behind it. He said, "Um... Ah, my name is, uh, Cliff, Clifford Hudson, and I, uh... My name is Clifford Hudson and I wish to confess my... Oh, God, please... I can't do this, goddamit..."

He started to sob. The voice from off-screen again: "No, no, no. Hud, *please*. We've been over this. My God, man, you only have three or four lines to say. Can you work with me here? Please? Just remember, this will be going out to a large television audience. Let that be your motivation. The whole city is watching, Hud."

The video camera swooped back suddenly and turned 180 degrees to reveal this man, Hudson, and another, fair-haired man: both naked but for their boxer shorts, tied together with what looked, oddly, like frilly women's underwear. They hung upside-down from a rope which, as seen through the lingering, crawling pan of the camera, trailed inside the apartment window across from the cameraman. It was impossible to tell how high it was, though the bodies seemed to be buffeted and jerked every few moments by strong winds.

The camera operator began to speak, a pastiche of the hushed tones of a nature documentary. Again, the voice was strange, a sort of residual buzz beneath the human tones.

"The yuppies often cling to one another for support in times of stress or danger. This species is renowned for its closeness and sense of solidarity. See how the dominant male asserts his authority and takes on the role of ambassador for the entire group…"

Hudson yelled out, "*Please*, you son of a bitch… Whaddyou *want* from us? Cut us down, for the love of Christ…"

The first voice, off-screen: "Cut you *down*? Ooh, I don't think you'd like that, Hud. That rope is the only thing keeping you *alive*." Then a directive, quieter: "Another foot."

The rope slipped, loosed outward by whoever controlled it inside the building, and the two men dropped like an elevator shaft, snapping to a stop. They screamed in unison and babbled across one another. The video abruptly cut to a man in a balaclava and nondescript charcoal-gray suit and tie, sitting in a very rough mock-up of a TV studio. Cardboard cut-outs behind him, the words "Karma TV" spray-painted in black; a desk made from a slab of pale, coarse wood. An old-style big band microphone, which looked real enough, sat on the desk. He shuffled some papers, rested his hands on the wood, cleared his throat—all the tics and routines of the average newscaster. Cathy, amused despite the gravity of the situation, dared not glance over at Jonathon to see if he recognized himself in any of this.

The man spoke: the voice first heard on the tape.

"Good evening, citizens, and welcome to Karma TV—where what goes around, comes around. And boy, *does* it come around. I trust we find you well. My name is Wilde and I'm joined tonight by my two companions..." The video cut to a still photo of a large man, in a balaclava and tuxedo, striking a declamatory, theatrical pose. "...Whitman..." Another cut, to a still shot of a smaller man in the same outfit, kneeling with a rose between his teeth and his hand held like an actor addressing Yorick's skull. "...and Waters."

It cut back to Wilde in the studio. He said, "Don't worry if you didn't catch that; the names are unimportant and, needless to say, not our own. What we're doing here, on the other hand, is all our own...and *very* important." He lifted a finger to the side. "Music, maestro."

Ladies' Night by Kool and the Gang began to play, a springy bass line and jaunty keyboards. Cathy caught Patrick's eye and smiled—half-bewildered but intrigued. Patrick shrugged and shook his head. One of the staffers started to wiggle his shoulders to the music. Bailey shot him a disapproving look.

"What?" the staffer said, as if caught off-guard by his superior's censure. "It's a good song."

The screen was now half-filled with a close-up on Wilde's masked face, saying, "Tonight was a very special night for one of our number here: Steven Ainsworth, who was celebrating his impending nuptials." A quick cut to old, black-and-white footage of a sentimental studio audience going "Aaw" in unison, then back to Wilde. "And, yes, there were ladies involved, so the significance of the words to the song is obvious. Two ladies, to be specific: the very lovely Amy and the very lovely, and very young, Dorothy." He began to sing: "'This is ladies' night, and the feeling's right...' Unfortunately, the feeling wasn't quite so right for Amy and Dorothy; in point of fact, they looked quite upset."

Cut to Waters softly strumming a Spanish guitar: "Traumatized, I would almost say, Wilde."

And back to Wilde: "Traumatized, yes. Excellent use of vocabulary there. Steven and his best man Hud, who you've already had the pleasure of meeting, decided to mark the beautiful occasion that is the union of man and woman by... Well. I don't want to go into too much detail—there may be children watching—but let's say their treatment of the lovely Amy and Dorothy was...less than chivalrous. In fact, it was downright nasty, and it makes me mad just thinking about it." He looked sharply to the side. "Another two feet."

The film cut to the two bound men as their rope slipped again, that vertiginous jolt. They screamed, together, at a surprisingly high pitch. Then the fair-haired one, Steven, lost control of his bladder; the soft stain of urine bloomed outward on his shorts before trickling down between their bodies.

Waters' voice was heard off-screen: "Uurgh! That is *disgusting*. Tsch. Some people..."

Cut back to the studio: "We've tried to get Steven and his pal to make amends and confess their sins. They know they've done wrong, I like to believe. They *want* to confess. They want to change." The masked face faded out, the picture refocusing as a super-fast, almost blurred montage of images: nude women in coy poses, fast sports cars, dollar signs, towering skyscrapers, handsome men maniacally laughing. Wilde continued in voiceover, "They want to leave behind the ignorant, misogynist assholes they once were, and be reborn. Innocent; pure; naked. But we seem to be having a slight problem with the confessions. Every time we ask them to speak, nothing but garbage comes out. Let's see if our viewers at home can understand."

The video returned to Hudson and Steven, half-choked by the straps and clasps of the underwear wrenched around their necks.

Hudson gasped, "Muh-my name is Clifford Hudson and I'm, I'm sorry… I wish to confess… Please. Let us *down*, goddamit…" He squinted at something being held in front of his face. "I confess to being a…a total jerk. I confess that I have used women as my playthings. I treated them like they were dog shit on my shoe. I've been… For God's sake, let us down…"

Steven said, "Oh shit. Whaddar we…? Oh shit, I'm sorry. My name is Steven Ainsworth and I'm sorry. I didn't mean it. Whaddar we gonna do, Hud? Oh shit. I, I, I've lived a disgusting, empty, worthless life. The world would be better off without…"

Back to Wilde, shaking his head. "Tut, tut. Not good enough, I'm afraid. Not *nearly* good enough. Anyway, this is where we're going to have to leave you, folks. Thanks for watching and, ah, sorry we couldn't have the sort of happy ending that I just *know* everyone out there wants to see. For Steve and Hud, I fear, the way is going to be a long and arduous one."

The picture cut to the two dangling men, terrified and piss-stained, swinging in the freezing night. Wilde said in voiceover, "But with our devoted help, and their newfound penitence for the revolting shit-heels they once were, I'm positive that redemption is near at hand. One way or another, none of us will be hanging around here for too long more."

Finally, the fade-out to a blank screen with flashing words: "Karma TV—coming to YOUR location. SOON."

Patrick exhaled heavily and leaned against the wall, eyes closed. Bailey dabbed at his forehead with a tissue, soaked through with sweat and discolored by the studio make-up melting from his face. George Oliver, who was stocky, balding, and incongruously good-looking, stood up and flicked on the main light.

He said, "Okay. First things first. A hoax? Or no? If no, are those two guys still alive someplace? When was this shot? Where? Was it in Manhattan? Will we be able to find them?" Facts and verities and what could be done; George was nothing if not a practical man, and besides this was an incurable optimist with a big heart.

"Holy shit. *That* was odd," Patrick said.

George handed his cell phone to a pretty young woman in combat trousers, her hair loosely bunched up. "Kyra—get the police over here. Pronto. Phone from in there." He turned to Cathy. "So whadda we do now, Cath? We can't use this shit, can we?"

"I don't… I don't know, George. Just…gimme a minute."

Bailey looked close to coronary arrest by now, his fingers splayed on his chest as he leaned forward in a plastic chair, staring vacantly into space. "Was I exaggerating? Did I exaggerate here? This is crazy stuff, crazy. It reminds me of all those goddamn militant groups in the seventies. Videotaped messages. Masked terrorists. Vague threats of more to come. Christ. And they send it to me. To *me*, for God's sake."

Patrick said, "So is that it? Terrorism? Is that what you guys think?"

"I don't know what to think about this, Patrick," Cathy replied. "Look, let's, ah… Everyone just clear out of here until the police arrive. Okay? Everyone clear out and leave the tape in the machine. Exactly the way it is. Who's handled it, anyway? Jonathon, it was delivered to you, right?"

"Yeah," Bailey said. "I took it out of the envelope. And then there was the kid I gave it to in here…"

He looked questioningly at George, who said, "Kyra. One of my team here. She's gone to call the cops."

"Right, Kyra. And that was it except for the goddamned courier… Wait a minute. Find the envelope. It might have a courier's stamp on it or something. We might…"

Cathy nodded, clapped her hands together twice, enthused now. "Yes. Good. They might have a record of whoever sent the tape in the first place. Could be something we can use there."

"Uh…I don't think so, Cathy." Patrick held up the padded

envelope—scuffed and dirtied from where it had lain on the floor—between his thumb and index finger, careful not to touch too much of it. "The couriers... They, ah, they won't be much help."

"You don't think so," Bailey said. "And why is that?"

"Because they don't exist."

He flipped the envelope around to reveal an ink stamp near the corner: "3W Courier Services: we help what goes around to come around."

Cathy whispered, "Three W's. Wilde, Waters, and Whitman. Isn't that what he said?"

Patrick nodded. George started shaking his head and chuckling softly.

"What is it, George?" Cathy asked. "What are you laughing at?"

He smiled wryly, shook his head again. "Karma TV. Goddamn it. That's pretty funny. If this whole thing wasn't so weird, I'd almost pitch it to the network myself."

NEW YORK HERALD-CHRONICLE   FRIDAY, JUNE 16TH

Man Forced to Assault Himself

by MARTINA McDONALD

Police in Brooklyn are investigating a bizarre incident that occurred two nights ago. Malcolm Strauss (51), an electrician, was watching television alone in his apartment, in the Cowden Heights complex on Prospect Street, at around 11pm when three masked men forced entry.

Mr. Strauss's wife, Helena (50), was staying with friends across town that evening.

According to police sources, the men stripped Mr. Strauss to his underwear and ordered him to punch his own face. When he refused, the gang dangled him upside-down outside his apartment window, 15 stories high.

The victim eventually relented and punched his own face some 20 times. He was subsequently taken to hospital for heavy bruising and a fractured knuckle, though his injuries are not thought to be serious.

NYPD Detective Audley Smith of the 84th Precinct, which is investigating the incident, commented: 'This has to be one of the oddest cases we've seen in some time.

'These guys basically broke in here, forced Mr. Strauss to beat himself up a little, then left without taking anything. We're baffled, but obviously will continue our investigations until the perpetrators are apprehended.'

It is also understood that, before leaving, the gang had spray-painted a message on Mr. Strauss's television screen: 'Suffer the slings and arrows...or take arms?'

Mr. Strauss, speaking on his return from hospital, said, 'What kind of psychos would do something like that, to a man in his own home? Your home is your castle, I've always believed that.

'And to make a man hit his own face like that, it's not right. Look at me, I'm a mess. I don't know why they picked on me, I never did anything to anybody.'

The investigation continues.

Chapter 3

The freaks are getting more inventive

THE heartbeat pulse of the cursor, the blurry, radioactive glow of the monitor, his fingers poised above the keys. He sighed heavily; the words weren't coming easily. He typed, "...and I said I was sorry and I meant it. I AM SORRY, GODDAMMIT. I don't know why I said all that stuff and you know I didn't mean it." He paused, re-read, deleted the last six words, and typed, "I know how much it hurt you."

Detective Sergeant Danny Everard screwed his eyes shut. That old child's trick: shut out the world for a few seconds in the quixotic hope that everything will be right by the time you open them. He looked at the screen again. It still didn't read quite the way he wanted, but it might have to do. Jesus—37 years old and getting tongue-tied yet by matters of the heart. He ran a hand down his lean face, then hesitantly grasped the mouse and directed it over the "Send" icon. He was about to click when his superior officer, Captain James Harte, opened the door of the small, tidy office in the Midtown South Precinct station and took a step inside.

"Danny? Excuse me. Are you in the middle of something?"

Danny whirled around, surprised. "Wha-? No, no. Just, ah... Nothing at all. Just sending an e-mail. What's up, Captain?"

"What's up? Ah, the usual. The days are getting shorter and the freaks are getting more inventive. They're not satisfied with just your average, common-or-garden crime any more. It's gotta *say* something now. Gotta look good for the cameras, right?"

Danny smiled. "I know this is leading somewhere, James."

Harte came into the center of the room. He cut an imposing figure, his broad shoulders and dark blue suit, his shaven head and trim moustache, skin like black silk over the characteristically elegant features of one of East African ancestry. Danny had always thought it very beautiful, that ebony-black skin; almost unreal, too perfect for the human animal. He sometimes compared it to his own wan complexion and jagged, blond hair, standing beside Harte before the expansive mirror of the men's room; he paled, literally, by comparison.

Harte said, "It certainly is. To be specific, it's leading you down to West 33rd. Network 4 studios. To talk with a..." He checked a piece of paper. "...Cathy Morrissey and a Jonathon Bailey. You know? The guy reads the headlines?"

"Talk about...?"

"A kidnapping. Some funny boys in balaclavas nabbed two yuppies and hung them from a high-rise apartment window. We don't know where yet. Balaclavas and evening dress, no less." Harte rubbed his eyes with his hand, rubbed his hand over his head. "Christ. What did I say about the freaks getting creative?"

"Actually, you called them 'inventive.' But what's all this got to do with a TV studio? What, did they offer Network 4 exclusive interview rights?"

Harte smiled, a big toothy grin. "Better. They sent them a tape of the whole thing. Videotape, old school."

Danny frowned in puzzlement, then shrugged and stood, lifting his jacket from the chair.

"Okay. I'll go check it out. This Bailey character and...?"

Harte handed him the paper with all the relevant information. "Morrissey. Cathy Morrissey. Head of the newsroom. The tape was sent to Bailey this morning. Three or four others watched it, but the two of them should be able to answer any questions about it."

"Right. Like, was it VHS or Betamax format?"

"Don't kid around with this, Danny. The whole thing smells like a college prank, but as far as I know, the people involved seemed genuinely scared. We might have a real abduction on our hands here. Alright? So don't kid around."

Danny wafted his hands up and down, a placating motion. "Don't kid around. I got it."

He moved toward the door, then spun around and returned to his desk. He clicked on "Send" and looked at the Captain. "Sorry. Some other serious business."

The air resistance outside the car audibly changed in pitch as Danny gained speed. He lit a cigarette and punched a number into his car phone. The muted burr of the dial tone rang out from the speaker, and then an impersonation of Christopher Lee, the venerable old movie star, on a comedy answering service: "*Hellooo*. This...is Christopher Lee. My good friend can't come to the phone right now—I have other plans for him—but leave a message...and he *may* get back to you... Ah ha ha ha *haaa*..."

Danny muttered, "Jesus Christ", then spoke more distinctly: "Look—it's me. Um...I don't really know what to say here. I've sent you an e-mail; maybe explains it better. God, I hate these fucking answering services. Feels like I'm talking into space. Which I am, right? Anyway... Listen. Read my mail, and have a think, and get back to me, okay? Please. We have to talk. I'm sorry, and I need to talk to you. ...Call me later. 'Bye."

He killed the connection and drove on, chewing on his lower lip and sucking hard on the cigarette.

The stench of Bailey's cigars had finally left the screening room, after heroic efforts by cleaning staff to freshen the air somewhat for the arrival of the NYPD. Danny was ushered inside by an obviously star-struck member of the security team, who had insisted on accompanying him the whole way there. Bailey sat at the wall farthest from the tape player, crossing and uncrossing his legs nervously, as Cathy stood, stretching her back. Her eyes were closed; she hadn't heard the soft click of the door opening. Danny leaned forward and cleared his throat.

Cathy opened her eyes, startled, staring at Danny for a moment. Then she smiled and said, "Oh. Hello. Sorry, I was just... Hi, how are you? Cathy Morrissey." She took his hand and shook it. "Detective Everard, isn't it?"

Danny felt for his badge. "Yeah, Danny Everard. Here's my, uh, my badge." He smiled. "You can check my credentials."

"Aw, there won't be any need for that."

Danny moved toward Bailey. "And this must be…Mr. Bailey, right?"

Bailey rose to meet him, shaking hands slowly, making a ceremony out of it. "Yes, that is I. Jonathon Bailey. You recognize me from television?"

"No, sir. I usually watch another channel."

Bailey pouted, a ludicrous expression for a man in late middle age. Cathy stifled a laugh.

"Alright, that's the introductions: why am I here?" Danny asked.

Bailey said, "You tell him. I just find the whole thing so…" He waved a hand, an oddly camp flutter.

Cathy sighed, like this was a story she knew would have to be told again and again. "Right. We got a package, okay—Jonathon, he got a package delivered this morning. Couriered. It's a videotape. It…appears to be footage of an abduction. As in, the aftermath of an abduction. There are two guys hung out of a window by these…what were the names again, Jonathon?"

"Ainsworth. Something Ainsworth and…I forget the other one."

"Steven. It was Steven Ainsworth. I'm not sure if we actually hear the second guy's name."

Danny said, "We might get it from the tape. So these two men had been abducted by person or persons unknown, hung outside a window and…what? Beaten? Tortured?"

"Um…I don't know. They didn't really look beat-up, although one of them had a bruise on his face. Like he'd been slapped, but maybe not punched. Or not hard anyway. They just sort of…hang there, you know? Oh, and I dunno if it's important, but they're wrapped up in lingerie."

Danny raised a skeptical eyebrow.

Cathy nodded and said, "Yep. Tied at the neck and wrists in Victoria's finest secret. And then Wilde comes on and starts talking about how he wants them to…"

He reached inside his jacket for a pen and notebook. "Hold on — what was that name?"

"Wilde. That's what he calls himself. The ring-leader. There's three of them: Wilde, Waters, and Whitman." She held up the courier package stamp to his face. "See? The 3Ws."

Danny frowned, thinking for a moment. "Okay. Maybe... I think I should probably look at this tape first."

Cathy nodded in agreement and moved off to ready the video recorder. He keyed a number into his cell phone.

"Kurt? Hi, Danny Everard here. Yeah, I'm okay, I'm good... Network 4 studios. What's that? Yeah, I wish... Listen, Kurt, I need a trace on a Steven Ainsworth." He turned to Cathy. "White?" She nodded again. "A young white male. We think lives in an apartment block — probably one of the better ones. Get back to me with a list of addresses, would you? The swankier the better. Okay? Thanks, man."

Danny crouched before the console as the video began to play, speaking softly into a Dictaphone, recording his first, intuitive impressions as the images popped up on screen.

"The gang seems to be professional; well-organized; clever; dangerous, I guess. Leader calls himself Wilde; his two accomplices are Whitman and Waters. Presumably some sort of joke reference to Oscar, Walt and...not sure about the last one. That film director? ...Tape is professionally edited and sound-tracked...some effort went into this. Their voices sound disguised; can't be sure. Not much to go on — yet."

He stood, nodding, with the Dictaphone to his mouth, a look of deep concentration. He began to chew on his lip again and mumbled, "Making a statement. Yeah. They're pissed about something and they want the public to know about it. Attention seekers. Definitely."

Cathy switched off the VCR and stood with hands on hips. "So whaddya think? Some weird shit, or what?"

Danny smiled. He looked about to speak when his phone

rang, a shrill, insistent tone. "Danny Everard... Kurt, thanks for getting back to me. Uh-huh... Tribeca...uh-huh... Hold on, lemme grab my pen. Alright, what's the full address? Uh-huh... They were having a party, right... Everyone left around two... Yep, sounds like the right area for our boys. Okay, have a car sent round. Whichever station is closest. I'll be there in less than an hour. And Kurt? Tell 'em to be careful—I don't know exactly what they're gonna find there."

He turned to Cathy and Bailey. "A few quick questions before I leave. Have there been any further communications—any ransom demands, threats, anything like that?"

Cathy said, "Nope. Nothin'. Nada. And so forth."

"Mr. Bailey—any idea why this was sent to you?"

Bailey shook his head. "No. None. I've never heard of this Steven Ainsworth, I don't know who he is, I don't know anything."

"Alright. Well, I think we can presume that you were chosen for your high profile...despite what I might have said 20 minutes ago."

Cathy smiled. She said, "I figured they want us to broadcast this. I mean, what other reason for making a recording in the first place? 'Cause you want people to see it."

"To pay attention. Right. While on the subject: I'm gonna have to prohibit that material from broadcast. Depending on what we find in this apartment, it could be evidence. And I'll need the tape."

Cathy went to the VCR and ejected the cassette. She said, "Don't worry. The brass already made that decision. They're probably scared in case it proves to be a hoax. Wouldn't wanna end up with egg on their faces, and all that."

Bailey swallowed heavily, wiping his forehead, and said, "Yes, you're welcome to it, Detective. And if I never see or hear of Karma goddamn Productions again, I'll die a happy man."

Danny moved toward the door, the videotape in his hand. He

stopped, one leg dragged back, a mime of stalled motion. "Yeah. I wish I could say that that's likely to be the case, Mr. Bailey, but… I dunno. We'll see."

Now, *this* was what you'd call a nice place. Danny stepped through heavy inner doors, one of which lay forlornly against the wall, its upper hinge twisted and buckled, and surveyed the scene. Apart from the door, and some upended furniture, the apartment was in surprisingly good condition, although evidence of a serious night's partying was scattered around—spilled food, bottles lying on the floor, indeterminate stains on the expensive rugs. And it was stunning: large, spacious, all clean lines and understated touches. Architect designed and professionally decorated. He assumed Mr. Ainsworth hadn't chosen the fabrics and furniture, anyway. This was like somewhere Peter might live—he'd have the money for it, almost, and certainly have the aesthetic sensibilities. Danny smiled to himself: on an NYPD detective's salary, today was about the nearest he'd ever come to basking in the splendor of a place like this.

He completed his circuit of the room. A length of strong rope, tied to a piano leg, led out an open window, the one on the tape. An evidence collection team was busy at various points, bending over or crouching down, scrabbling around for evidence, for physical matter, like white-clad ants methodically going about their business. Danny admired the techs their dedication, their single-mindedness, that unlearned ability to focus on one tiny but hugely important thing. He fixed on the far corner, where the two abductees sat wrapped in blankets, sipping coffee. They were still stripped to their underpants, and looked physically and emotionally wiped-out, especially the fairer one, who babbled even more incoherently than on the video. A crescent-shaped bruise was turning dark along the length of his cheek.

An officer surprised Danny as he turned back to the main part of the room, making him jump a little despite himself. "Sorry to have startled you, sir. Officer Churchill, First Precinct. We're, ah, we're the nearest station, sir."

Danny said, amused, "Churchill? Like the British politician?"

"Yes, sir. The funny thing is, I'm not actually of British descent at all. I'm half German and one third Portuguese. Not too sure about the rest of it."

"I won't even ask where the name came from. What's the story here, Officer?"

Churchill blew out his cheeks, readying himself for the telling. "We got here about 50 minutes ago, sir. Secured the scene, called for a CSU team. Those two gentlemen were tied together on the rug in the corner. Both naked almost, bound at the ankles, wrists, and neck by, uh, by ladies' underwear, sir. Heavy duct tape underneath; a bitch to cut off." He leaned in close, obscuring his voice from the two men on the ground. "They seem okay—physically, I mean—but we're checking them for exposure and hypothermia. Apart from some burns and tearing on the legs and feet, they haven't got any serious wounds to the body. But, ah…they're pretty fucked-up in the head, sir, excuse the old language. Especially the fairer one."

"Excused. When will they be ready to talk?"

"We're just feeding and dressing 'em now, sir. Give us five minutes and they're all yours."

"Good job, Officer Churchill. I can see you going places in the world."

Churchill smiled, a funny, innocent pride on his face. "Like into politics, sir?"

Danny smiled too and moved to the window. He lit a cigarette without thinking and checked his cell phone for messages—there were none. He caught his reflection in the window: the long hooked nose, the deep-set eyes. He'd often been told he looked like Daniel Day-Lewis, except maybe ten years younger, and he could see the resemblance, sometimes. It was the nose, he decided; that, and the way his overall look, despite his blond hair, had always cast something of a dark shadow.

His reverie was disturbed by a shout: "Hey! Hey, you. Who said you could smoke in here?"

He turned to where the dark-haired fellow sat up, dressed now though still shoeless, glaring at him, a fire in his eyes. Danny had to hand it to him: a night of trauma and catastrophe, and the guy was still willing to be bellicose with a cop he'd never met before.

He walked over, still carrying his cigarette, and said, "Mr. Ainsworth?", realizing in that split-second that he'd mixed the names up.

"No, I'm not Mr. fucking Ainsworth. *That's* Steve. I'm Clifford Hudson, and I asked you who said you could smoke here."

Danny looked to the paramedic tending the two, who shrugged and said, "He's been like that since we got here. He's pissed over...*something*."

Hudson exploded in angry laughter. "Ha! *Pissed*!? You think so, genius? Christ. You're goddamned *right* I'm pissed. I've been lying on this fucking rug freezing for eight hours." He glared at Danny. "And where the fuck were you assholes all night?"

Danny said, "We got here as soon as possible, Mr. Hudson. Now, you need to calm down and..."

"I will *not* fucking calm down!" He stopped, thinking. "I knew it. Not one of those bastards called you. You only just found out about this, right? We had 45 people here last night, and they all saw what happened, and not *one* of those motherfuckers called the cops!"

Danny crouched down, half-wondering what he was going to do with that cigarette. He fixed his trousers over his thighs and said, "Why do you think that might be the case, sir?"

"Well, they..." Hudson looked away, his bravado mingling with something else; something quieter, less assured. "How the hell should I know? You're the fucking cop, go do your job. Shut *up*, Steve."

Ainsworth was rambling again, swaying beneath the blanket and still shivering, despite the fact that the paramedic had by now helped him to put on trousers, a shirt, and a heavy sweater. He had tears in his eyes, or else it was sweat trickling down from his hairline.

"We...we didn't hurt 'em," he mumbled. "Look, they're okay. It was all his idea... Look, you can see they're not hurt..."

The paramedic said, "He might be in shock. I'd better take him to the hospital, just to be sure."

Danny nodded, and the paramedic lifted Ainsworth from the ground, gingerly, and led him away by the elbow.

"Okay, Mr. Hudson," Danny said. "Feel up to answering a few questions?"

"I don't see why... Yes, godammit. Ask your questions and let me the fuck out of here."

Danny stubbed out the cigarette in a plant pot and the two men moved to the low coffee table, settling into luxuriant sofas. Danny pulled out a notebook and poised with his pen.

"Alright. Let's start at the start. How did these men enter the apartment?"

"They...someone must have buzzed them through the outer doors. With the electronic security lock. One of us at the party. When they reached here, they just...kicked the fucking thing off of the hinges, I don't know."

"How many were they?"

"Three. One of them was really big. They went by code-names, you know? What was it? Wilde..."

"...Waters and Whitman."

Hudson looked up, surprised. "Yeah. That was exactly it."

"Okay. Were they armed?"

"Yeah, they had, uh, pistols. With silencers. They each had a bag, too, so I dunno...could have had more shit in there, I guess."

Danny pressed on, scribbling furiously. He'd have to decipher that spidery scrawl later, which would be a royal pain in the ass, but right now the momentum was important—get Hudson to lock onto his memories, all of them, even the ones he didn't realize he held.

"Good. Did you notice anything about them? A voice, an accent, something you might recognize?"

"Nah, their voices were…just regular voices, I guess. No particular accents. They were kinda…deep, or… They were muffled anyway, by the, uh, the hoods they wore."

"Regular voices. And they all wore a tuxedo, and a balaclava on the head?"

"Balaclava, that's right. We could just see, like, their eyes and mouths. Nothing else."

"That's a pity… Okay, so they burst in here, they stripped you, they tied you up in…in, whatever…and hung you outside the window. Correct?"

Hudson glowered again. "Yes. Jesus, do we really have to go through all the tiny fucking details over and over?"

"Just once should do it. So what then? Did they beat you, hurt you, what? What did these men actually do to your friend and you?"

The young man leaned back into the plump cushions, dropped his head over the couch's headrest. He groaned quietly, and resurfaced with a glaze of extreme fatigue like a shroud over his face.

"They…didn't really *do* anything," he said. "It was weird, okay? I was wiped out; I'd had a lot to, uh, to drink. They just strung us up and asked us things, about ourselves, and what we were doing last night. And they made us, like, defend ourselves, and read stuff off cards. Confession, that's what they called it. Motherfuckers. Thought they were in a goddamn courtroom. Or a church."

"And that was it? Just questions?"

"Pretty much. They let the rope slip a few times—trying to scare us, I guess, and it fucking worked. I can tell you, man, I was terrified. Steve went completely. Pissed down on both of us a few times. But other than that they didn't hurt us, no. Just...talked. And asked their goddamn questions."

Danny squeezed the bridge of his nose. He paused, bracing himself for this question.

"Okay. That's about it. Just one last question, Mr. Hudson—why you?"

"Why me what?"

"Why you and your friends? Why did they target this particular party?"

Hudson's belligerence flared again, like the sulfurous yellow of a match head. He shouted, "Hey, what is this shit? 'Why us?' How the fuck should I know?"

Danny kept his voice low and calm, but insistent—Hudson had to know who had the power here. "Calm down, Mr. Hudson. I'm just trying to work out if maybe you knew these guys, if there was some sort of personal vendetta going on..."

Hudson sat up, tried to stand, fell back into a sitting position again. He said, "Get the fuck outta my face, okay? How should...? ...Look, I don't... We didn't know them, okay? I haven't got a fucking clue why they picked on us, but I don't *know* them."

Danny stared at him; held the stare, made the other man's eyes come around to meet his. He said, "Okay. They must have had their own reasons, then."

Hudson looked pointedly at the waxed wooden floors. "Yeah, that's it. Their own reasons. Now why don't you stop treating me like *I'm* the goddamned criminal instead of the victim." His eyes rose once more—there was that fire again. "*They* assaulted *us*, for Christ's sake!"

Danny stood and gathered his things from the table. "You can, ah, rest assured—*sir*—that these men will be subject to the full rigor of the law when they are apprehended."

He moved off, Hudson calling in his wake: "Ah, stick your

fucking smart talk, okay, pal? Who are you to judge me anyway…?"

The forensics people had set up equipment at the other corner of the room. Danny strolled over, feeling irate and strung-out and weirdly conflicted, and flashed his badge at the team leader, a portly man in his fifties with graying, wavy hair which flowed over the collar of his jacket.

Danny said, "Detective Sergeant Everard, Midtown South. Would I be way off the mark in guessing that you haven't found anything much?"

"Bill Rosenberg—good to meet ya. No, you'd be pretty much exactly *on* the mark. No prints that stand out, no physical evidence left lying around… There are fibers, of course, but those could belong to our three fun boys, or Prince Charming over there and his pals last night."

"Oh, so you've met the lovely Mister Hudson, then?"

Rosenberg glanced across the room, still scribbling something in a small box on the top page of his clipboard. "Yeah—a *real* beauty. We'll take fiber samples and analyze them anyway, but don't hold your breath."

"Shit. That's it?"

"Not quite. We also found…" Rosenberg gestured to one of his team. "Hey! Maria! Bring that over here, please."

Maria was young, dark, and sweet-faced, with enormous brown eyes. An Old World sort of look. She handed Rosenberg a sealed plastic bag and smiled pleasantly at Danny.

"Alright, Maria, alright. Run along," Rosenberg said. "You can flirt with Detective Everard *after* work."

She rolled her eyes indulgently and left. Danny smiled, a little embarrassed. He said, "Um… So, uh, so what is it?"

The forensics expert handed him the bag and a pair of surgical gloves. "It's a card. Found it in that crystal bowl over there on the table."

Danny put on a glove and gingerly lifted the card out. It was coated in a fine dust. He touched his left little finger to the dust and then to his tongue.

"Have your team check the bowl for traces of cocaine," he said, looking back at a sheepish Hudson. "No rule against investigating two crimes at once, right?"

Rosenberg smiled. Danny examined the card: plain, clean-edged, off-white or ivory in color. Hand-written, in neat block capitals, was "YOU DIDN'T THINK WE WERE GOING TO KILL THEM, DID YOU?", followed by a line in quotation marks, which he read aloud: "'...with the absolute heart of the poem of life butchered out of their own bodies.' Hmm."

"Very moving. What is that?"

"I know this. It's Allen Ginsberg. Part of *Howl*. Near the end, I think."

"Another 'berg', huh? Well, I can't fault their taste."

Danny flicked the card gently with his gloved fingers. "No. Me neither. Keep me posted, would you?"

Rosenberg said, "No problem", and returned to his painstaking, intricate, fascinating work.

NEW YORK HERALD-CHRONICLE   MONDAY, JULY 9TH

Heinemann House, Cars Destroyed by Mindless Vandals

by SIMON MERRILL

Security has been stepped up around the home of Judge Karl Heinemann (60), a colorful member of the judiciary for the past 25 years, after his house and cars were vandalized in an apparently random attack.

Judge Heinemann, his wife and their two children were attending a gala performance at the New York City Ballet when the incident took place. His house staff had been given their monthly night off.

According to police sources, the perpetrator entered by a ground-floor window at the back of the 12-bedroom house, located on fashionable Park Avenue.

Once inside, they poured concentrated acid over furniture, antiques, electronics, floor coverings, and clothes, though items in the bedrooms of the Judge's two young daughters (aged 8 and 10) were left untouched.

The perpetrator then forced entry to Judge Heinemann's garage, where they poured acid over his collection of vintage cars, including a Rolls Royce Silver Spirit.

NYPD Detective Thom Putnam, of the 23rd Precinct, which is handling the investigation, said that nothing had been taken in the attack, adding, 'Nothing was moved out of place, either.

'It was all just destroyed where it stood. Armchairs, antique mirrors, clothes hanging in the wardrobe.

'We suspect this was a convicted felon who may have a grudge against Judge Heinemann for a sentence handed down, and are following a definite line of inquiry.'

Detective Putnam also confirmed that a message had been left by the perpetrator, scorched into the ceiling with gasoline. The

(cont'd next page)

Heinemann (cont'd)

message read, 'You were right: temptation IS hard to resist.'

This is thought to be a reference to last month's controversy involving the Judge, in which he handed down a six-month suspended sentence for a rape conviction, and declared that the victim's dress and behavior on the night in question had possibly 'tempted' the convicted man. Women's groups and rape crisis centers reacted angrily to his comments.

Now Judge Heinemann has increased security around his home and garden. He is understood to have employed the services of Fortress Security, a specialist company that has provided a former Secret Service operative as the Judge's personal bodyguard. Meanwhile, the investigation continues.

Chapter 4

Love awaits

DOYLE'S was warm, dark, welcoming, and very crowded. Raucous folk-rock thumped through the walls and vibrated on the street outside as Patrick approached. He stopped for a moment in the doorway, scanning the posters for forthcoming musical attractions and big-screen sporting events. Bright highlighter marker, glossy white paper. Tonight, he saw, Doyle's would be "rocking to the Celtic fusion sounds of The Ribbonmen, New York's finest Irish pub band." He smiled skeptically and went inside.

Drums snapped, guitars twanged, and a fiddle wheeled around the melody, a juiced-up version of the old folk standard, *The Raggle Taggle Gypsy*. Through the mass of people he just about saw Cathy standing at the bar, drinking beer from the bottle, and nodding her head to the music. Beside her was a tall, serene-looking gentleman who Patrick assumed to be her husband Philip. They looked a little odd together, the variance in height and body shape, but sort of cute, too. Patrick passed the band in the corner, all straggly hair and flared, retro trousers, the lead singer rattling a tambourine like a shaman warding off ill fortune. He struggled through the crowd and finally reached Cathy, shouting to be heard.

"Hey! Sorry I'm late."

Cathy smiled in greeting and shouted back, "Hi there. What?"

"I *said*… Listen. It's kinda loud in here. Can we go to a table?"

"Huh?"

Patrick smiled hello to Philip, then pointed toward the far corner, a vacant table nestled beneath warped wooden shelves holding dusty old bottles. Cathy shrugged in agreement. Philip tilted his head in the direction of the bar and mouthed the word, "Beer?" Patrick nodded and mouthed, "Thanks." Then Cathy took his hand and led him through the crowd. He slumped into the seat, the noise receded somewhat, muffled by a wall of people and the stairway passing over their heads.

He said, "That's a bit better. Jesus, this place is *loud*."

"Ah, don't be such a wuss. This is what's called atmosphere, darling."

Patrick laughed. "I should have known better than to meet you in an Irish bar. Are they all like this?"

She said, deadpan, "Yes, Patrick. We Irish listen to this type of music all the time. We're like the world's kings and queens of drinking and carousing. Seriously."

He punched her playfully on the shoulder as Philip returned with the drinks, clutched in his large hands. He carefully lowered them onto the table and leaned over to shake Patrick's hand, saying, "How are you? Philip Genet. Cathy's better half."

Cathy said, "And *such* a better half, darling. This is Patrick. I mentioned him earlier?"

Patrick stood into the shake and said, "Hi, Philip. Good to finally meet the man brave enough to commit himself to this tyrant."

He returned to his seat, where Cathy returned the punch. Philip drank a healthy measure of beer, the foamy head forming a thin moustache which he licked clean, and said, "So whereabouts you from, Patrick? Are you local here?"

"Yep, born and bred a city boy. I was in LA for five years — university first and then dicking around for a while. Traveled abroad a bit. Came back to New York when I got the Network 4 job a few months ago."

"Where are you staying, actually?" Cathy said.

"My folks' old place. Upper west side. They retired two years ago; on one of those world tour things ever since."

"Oh, that's nice."

"Yeah. Then there's only my sister Marie, and she's married in Canada, so...I sort of have the place to myself."

"And that's even nicer."

Philip leaned across the table, resting his arms on it, saying, "So, Patrick, tell me about this thing today. This videotape. Cathy said it was something pretty weird."

Patrick sighed and took a sip from his drink. "Yeah, well... It was sorta strange, alright. It was...hard to describe, really."

"Got Bailey pretty spooked," Cathy said.

"There's a tragedy, huh? Nah, I'm kidding... I think we should just leave it with the cops, you know? They're the experts."

Philip nodded in understanding and rose from the table. "Probably can't say too much, right? I understand." He turned to Cathy. "I'm just gonna check on the babysitter."

She made a face, a sort of affectionate reproach, and Philip waved his hands. He said, "No, no, she's young. I'm not doubting her, I'm just...checking in. Back in a tick."

Patrick and Cathy sipped their beers for a few moments, not speaking. A cheer rose from the crowd on the completion of the song, and Cathy touched Patrick's hand, a concerned look behind the reflection on her spectacles.

"Patrick, seriously: what did you think of that today?"

He shook his head slowly. "I don't know, Cath. I honestly don't. Like I said, it was...strange."

"But do you think there's gonna be more? I mean, are we being dragged into something here? And Jonathon. I know you don't like him—Jesus, I can't *stand* him half the time—but I don't like this. The fact that they addressed it to him. I know what that detective said, but..."

Patrick crossed his legs, turning toward her. He placed a hand on her shoulder and said, "I wouldn't worry about it. I think your cop friend was right. They picked him 'cause he's a name, you know? The famous Jonathon Bailey. Who better to...to get the message across, or whatever?"

"I hope you're right. I don't want any of us getting involved in this."

He gazed into the crowd, mulling it over, focusing his thoughts by distracting the senses. He said eventually, "As far as I can tell, none of us are. Not directly, anyway. They're using us as a...what? A medium or something, but it doesn't have anything to do with us." Patrick squeezed her hand firmly. "Trust me, Cath: none of us is going to get hurt. Okay?"

She nodded and smiled, fears a little relieved but not banished completely. The band had launched into a hectic, electric rendition of a plaintive ballad when Philip returned and gave a thumbs-up, just as Patrick stood and grabbed his bag.

Philip said, "Everything ship-shape and A-OK. I said she was a good kid. Hey, you're not leaving, are you?"

Patrick slugged down the end of his beer. "Yep. Got to, I'm afraid."

Cathy smiled at him, teasing. "Hot date?"

"Hey, what can I tell you?" he said, grinning broadly. "I'm young, free, and good-looking. The city is alive, and love awaits."

Night in the city, and the beautiful people were at play. That is to say, most of the men in this particular Greenwich Village club were beautiful, which made Benjamin Van Horne—almost 40, short-legged, with thinning hair and a weak chin—feel less attractive than usual. But his physical inadequacies didn't seem to matter to the wildly handsome young guy dancing opposite him, hands locked above his head as he jerked his hip sideways to the pulsing music.

Christ, he really is stunning, Benjamin thought, as the strobe lights scanned down his dance partner's dark skin, his lithe, muscular physique. The man pursed his lips and laughed, closed his eyes, ran his hands along the mesh fabric of his tight-fitting top. Benjamin shuffled his feet and clicked his fingers, a little self-conscious, a large part disbelieving. The guy was definitely interested, and Benjamin could scarcely accept it. He wasn't ugly, he didn't think, but this vision of male loveliness was in another universe to his level. And yet, and yet... Here they were, flirting, dancing, moving closer and backing away, those little matador rhythms of seduction. The other man hooked his fingers around

Benjamin's tie and began leading him from the dancefloor as the tune segued into a slower song. Benjamin smiled dumbly, stopping just short of pinching himself, and thought, Welcome to your lucky day, Van Horne. Now shut up and enjoy it.

They reached the bar and found their drinks. Benjamin said, projecting his voice over the music, "So, ah, sorry, I couldn't hear your name properly earlier."

"Tommy. What's yours?"

"Benjamin. Benjamin van Horne. I'm a stockbroker."

Tommy wiped the sweat from his forehead with an elegant stroke of his finger, saying, "Sounds fascinating."

Benjamin smiled, bashful and self-aware. "Afraid not. The money's good, though. Paid for that sweet little number I pulled up in. And business makes a handy excuse for…uh…for when…"

"So you're married, obviously."

Benjamin looked away, toward the dancefloor, guilt passing over his face in the sweep of the lights. He said, "Yeah. You're not pissed at that, are you? I mean, I know a lot of you don't like guys like me. I've been called a tourist plenty times. But it's not like that."

Tommy smiled. "'Course it isn't, Ben. Nah, I don't mind at all."

"Great. Excellent."

Tommy touched a slender hand to Benjamin's face, his throbbing temple, beating an infinitesimal tattoo. He ran his hand down to Benjamin's chin and said, "In actual fact, Ben, I find it a bit of a turn-on sometimes. You know, thinking about the little wifey at home all the time we're…"

Benjamin squirmed but didn't pull out of the embrace. "Uh…I dunno. I can get pretty guilty about it, I gotta say. I mean, she thinks I'm at a conference for the next two days, and here I am."

"Listen. Why don't you put wifey to the back of your mind for an hour or two? I know a safe little spot we can go to. You can feel guilty tomorrow."

He raised an eyebrow and touched Benjamin's lower lip, the heavy silver ring on his middle finger glinting in a spotlight. Benjamin smiled widely.

"Well, hell. Why not? What she doesn't know can't hurt her, right?"

"Can't hurt her. Exactly. Meet me around the side in five minutes."

Tommy pushed with his thumb, gently, into Benjamin's lip, then turned and walked off into the crowd. Benjamin checked his watch, checked his pulse rate, and finally checked his hair in the full-length bar mirror. Hey, you're not so bad-looking, he said to himself. In this light, anyway. He took a deep, steadying breath, fixed his jacket against his neck and left, his squat reflection matching his progress, rippling beside him in silver and glass.

He wasn't an especially courageous man and wasn't known to take risks, and Benjamin's excitement was commingled with a low trepidation as he peered into the dark alleyway beside the club. A neon sign saying Klub Khan was mirrored in a dirty puddle at the mouth of the alley. A streetlight cast a wan, dirty-yellow glow a little of the way in. Benjamin was hesitant.

He called out, "Uuh...Tommy? Are...are you there, Tommy?"

Then Tommy appeared from behind the far corner, his face illuminated by the flare of a cigarette lighter. He lounged against the wall, beautiful, cat-like, languorous, and beckoned Benjamin with his finger.

"C'mon, Mr. Stockbroker. Come with me and forget about everything."

Benjamin grinned, the tension easing out, and started to walk down the alleyway toward Tommy, who loitered at the corner for a moment before turning on his heel and motioning Benjamin to follow. The well-dressed stockbroker sauntered after him, passing through a small area of almost perfect darkness and entering a reasonable-sized yard. Benjamin guessed this was the rear of the club, a storage area or something. He stepped into an elongated pool of light cast by a lamp. Tommy was at the pool's outer edges, hip cocked, drawing slowly on his cigarette. Although he had done this before, a few times, Benjamin suddenly felt a little stupid.

He said, "So, uh...should I just whip it out, or what? Wha-what do you wanna do?", and began laughing nervously.

Tommy smiled. "What do I wanna do? Well, Ben, I think I wanna do...*you*."

He whistled and three men stepped out of the darkness, forming a sort of crescent. Strangely, even while his legs were turning to jelly as he realized he'd been set up, Benjamin noted that the gang was comprised of four distinct ethnicities: black, white, Hispanic, and Asian. He raised his hands in protest.

"No, no. Wait. Hold on there. Just... Tommy, please. What are you doing? I thought..."

Tommy laughed, his big, brilliant teeth white against the night. "You *thought*? You didn't fucking think, Ben. You didn't think at *all*."

The gang rushed forward, kicking and punching Benjamin, spitting out insults. Bare fists and boots only, but Benjamin had a dread certainty that they weren't going to stop at that. Tommy remained outside the scuffling circle, dancing around gleefully, Mohammed Ali skips and little air-punches. He lit another cigarette and came closer, drawing random kicks at Benjamin's body as his men moved aside.

Tommy said, "You didn't *think*, Ben. You didn't use your faggot-assed little brain in there, my man. What, you thought a guy like me was gonna put out for a disgusting fuck like you?"

Benjamin was on his knees, mumbling through a bloodied mouth, "Please. My wife...she doesn't know. I can't have her find out. Please, Tommy. Why are you doing this...?"

A couple wandered down the alleyway, arms around one another's waists, seeking a private spot. They stopped, shocked, eyes rolling from Benjamin to the gang members. Tommy snarled at them and they fled, and Benjamin knew that he wouldn't live the night.

Tommy leaned over him, affecting a whining tone of voice, saying, "'My wife doesn't know, my wife doesn't know.' Well, she's *gonna* know, Benny boy. So why don't *you...*" He kicked, hard, to the face. "...have a *think...*" Another kick, to the chest. "...about *tha-*"

Then everything went sort of funny for Benjamin, struggling to see through his tears and the jolts of endorphins flooding his body. As Tommy drew back his leg a chain snaked out of the darkness and looped around the bastard's calf, pulling it from under him and sending him crashing to the ground. His friends whirled around to see three men in tuxedos and balaclava masks, standing together, a tight military formation. Whitman dangled a length of heavy chain from his huge fist.

A greasy-haired white guy in denim jacket and ponytail said, "What the fuck is this?"

Wilde stepped forward, hands behind his back. "'Love may be blind, but love at least knows what is man and what mere beast...' So which are you? Man or beast?"

Tommy stood and brushed the dust off his jacket. He wiped blood from his mouth and grinned, a horrible expression, vicious and uncontrolled. "What's that supposed to mean, faggot?"

Wilde said, "It's called poetry. You should try it sometime. Open your mind. Now, the rest of you—step away from that man."

"You broke some of my teeth, bitch," Tommy said. "I'm gonna fucking *bleed* you for that."

Whitman said, "Actually, that was me. See?", and waggled the chain.

"Yeah. That was you, ha ha. Funny guy. Real...fucking...*funny!*"

On that beat he lunged at Whitman, his long arms stretching

for the chain; and a beat later, as if it were a choreographed move, the rest of the gang jumped Wilde and Waters. Benjamin rolled away into the background, scared and bleeding, as Whitman drove Tommy's head into a chain-link fence. It rattled with the impact, a cymbal sound; the metal bent but didn't tear. Tommy's hand was like a claw behind him, grabbing for the chain. Wilde parried the blows of a slim, tall Asian man, blocking them with his forearms, then smacked his ears and struck a sharp, thin blow to the throat. The man choked for air and staggered backward. Wilde turned to where Waters struggled, outnumbered and outweighed, by the guy with the ponytail and a muscular Latino man. They each landed a punch on Waters' lower body before Wilde sprinted over, kicking one in the back and sending him sprawling, arms outstretched, into a muddy puddle. Waters pummeled the white guy with a volley of punches, his opponent's head snapping back, a thin squirt of blood from his nose into the air. Ponytail blinked, a patina of oblivion passing over his face, and fell to the ground.

Tommy and Whitman were still locked together, slamming into the fence, scrabbling for purchase in the dirt. Whitman grabbed him in a headlock, drove his powerful fist into the thug's face, three, four times. The Asian and Hispanic men stumbled away, toward the darkness and escape, as Tommy wrenched himself from Whitman's arm-lock and dashed for the alleyway...and ran straight into Waters' tensed fist. He dropped, out cold. Waters winced and flexed his fingers.

Benjamin drew himself into the fetal position and looked up, nervously, at the three masked figures standing over him.

"You...you're not going to hit me, are you? I mean...I kinda figure you're on my side."

Wilde stretched out his hand. "Get up. Come on, take my hand."

Benjamin stood and brushed himself down, then began gingerly touching his face for signs of damage. He pressed his fingers to his cheek, pummeled and bruised the color of uncooked meat, and said, "Ouch. Jesus, that *hurts*. That treacherous little shit. He loosened some teeth here..." He looked at the three men again. "So, uh...who are you guys anyway? What, ah...why did you help me?"

Waters and Wilde smiled at each other in unison, a snap recognition, that unspoken communication between old friends. Waters said, "Go on, you say it. Corny one-liners were always more your thing."

"In your case, sir," Wilde said, "let's just say we're your very own personal tooth fairies."

Whitman crouched over Tommy, groggily coming around, and placed a damp handkerchief to his mouth, holding it there until the reflexive, sluggish kicking stopped. He began tying the man's hands. Benjamin took a step toward the streetlight and staggered, moaning woozily.

Wilde said, "Are you okay? Do you think you need a doctor?"

"Yeah. A fucking *head* doctor. I gotta be crazy. Tell me what I should say to my wife when I get home."

"You're married?" Waters said.

"Aw, not you as well. Yeah, I'm married, okay? I'm married and I'm gay and I cheat on my wife with other men. And no, I'm not proud of it, if that's what you want to hear."

"Hey, it's your life, mister. We're not in the business of judging others...well, 'cept for your friend there."

"Tommy? I only met him tonight. He hit on me in the club. Ha. Hit on me. God, I'm so stupid."

Whitman bent his knees, braced himself and hoisted Tommy onto his back in one smooth sweep. The gang started to walk away, then Wilde stopped and faced Benjamin.

"Look, for what it's worth... Tell your wife. Tell her you're gay, or bi, or whatever it is you think you are. As a wise man once said, truth is beauty and true love more beautiful still; if her love is true she'll forgive you."

He turned to go. Benjamin called out, "Who wrote that? Tennyson?"

Wilde smiled back at him. "Nah. Wilde. The second version."

Darkness. Soft music played on the vehicle's stereo—Elvis Presley crooning *Blue Moon*, that sparse, mournful sound—accompanied by the whoosh of the road rushing by underneath.

Tommy awoke and tried to shake the fuzz from his head. He scrunched up his nose, and felt a sharp pain between his eyes. It'd better not be broken, he thought, all mashed out of shape, or that big fucker in the hood was going to pay. His eyes came into focus on something dark and formless. His vision blurred and sharpened again, and he saw the one with the red bow tie sitting across from him, reading a book, a thin paperback. Tommy yelped involuntarily; Wilde looked up and smiled, giving him an ironic army salute, a slow sweep of his pointed hand. Then Tommy realized that he couldn't move his arms. He looked down, agitated—he was naked, bound hand and feet in duct tape.

He yelled, "Hey. Hey, what the…? Get this shit offa me, man! Let me outta here!"

Tommy banged his head off the side of the van; Whitman, driving, turned up the radio volume in response.

"Aaargh!! Someone get me *outta* here! Help! Somebody! You creepy son of a bitch, lemme *go*, goddamit! You…motherfucker…I'll…"

He strained against his binds, shoulders pushed back to the point of discomfort, and tried to charge at Wilde, butting like a stag. Wilde rose smartly and slammed him back against the side of the van. Waters placed a silenced handgun to Tommy's temple.

Tommy said, "Whaddar you…? Okay. Okay, I get it. This is because of…back there, right? Okay. That's cool. Just listen to me, man—those fags, they get what's coming…"

Wilde placed a finger to Tommy's lips. "Hush. You talk too

much, Tommy."

Waters said, "Empty vessels, Wilde."

Wilde pulled a blindfold from his jacket pocket and began tying it around Tommy's head. Tommy squirmed away, his bare backside scratched from the rough curved metal on which he sat, and said, "Hey, whoa. Not a blindfold. You don't need a blindfold, man..."

"*Hush*, Tommy. You'll get your chance to talk," Wilde said. "And you should think about what you're going to say." He leaned in close, dropping his voice to a whisper. "Like others before you, you're going to be remembered for this—so think carefully."

Darkness again, but this time with tiny, pulsing whiteness at the bottom of the screen: "Karma TV. A 3W Production." Just above it, a message scrolled once from right to left: "NOTICE: This film is for educational purposes only. All copyright is protected. Our lawyers are watching" with an acid-house smiley face as a large period. Then the blank screen faded away to a shot of Wilde, against a blank background, wearing a surgical smock and his balaclava. The effect was simultaneously silly and unnerving. He spread his arms out wide.

"Good evening once again, citizens, and welcome to the second installment in our series of educational programming. Actually, scratch that—it's more *re*-educational. A sort of de-learning and then re-learning. The first program went quite well, anyway—one or two lessons have been absorbed by our subjects."

The video cut to footage of John Wayne in his heyday, that brash, weatherworn face; then a gruesome bare-knuckle boxing match and cheery marchers in a gay pride parade.

Wilde said, in voiceover, "We come to you tonight from the pleasant surrounds of the Enforced Karma Clinic for Inveterate Homophobes: where we delve deep into the dark, sticky unconscious of the real man's man. And tonight's subject is…homosexuality."

It cut to an actor with a melodramatically shocked expression, then back to the parade: mainly men, though a few women, in gaudy costumes, hoisting placards and waving to the crowd, blowing kisses, acting it up. An enormous man in a feather headdress and gold bikini danced badly to whatever music was accompanying the event. He noticed the camera on him and waved extravagantly.

The voiceover continued: "I know, I know. A lot of people out there aren't too happy with the notion of two men getting all— ooh, you know—*dirty* together."

Cut to Waters posing with a confused expression, saying, "But what is this 'homosexuality' all about, Wilde? And why does it upset people so?"

Then Wilde, holding an encyclopedia, leafing through its pages. "I'm glad you asked, Waters. From the *World Book* encyclopedia, 1986 edition: 'Causes of homosexuality are not fully understood. According to the most widely accepted theory…' Nah, that's boring. Ah, here's something: 'Most homosexuals appear no different from other members of their own sex.' Well, how about that?"

The video switched to a shot of a woman fainting in shock, then back to Wilde as he strolled down a dark, deserted corridor, arms behind his back like a pompous college professor. His white smock shone in contrast to the dank, damp walls, streaked a horrible color with the run-off of decades of leaks.

"To be honest, folks, homosexuality really doesn't mean anything either way. It just *is*. And what's wrong with that?" Cut to Whitman shrugging his shoulders, and back to Wilde again. "But here's a thing: up to ten per cent of the population is believed to have gay or bisexual leanings. Think on that—ten per cent. If the average person knows, say, 200 people reasonably well, around 20 of those close acquaintances are likely to be—

gasp!—*deviants*. Weird. Perverted. Not normal. And so on."

Then a succession of images, still and moving, of famous gay or bisexual men and women from history: from Socrates, Alexander the Great, Leonardo da Vinci, and Pedro Almodóvar to Virginia Woolf, Martina Navratilova, Frida Kahlo, and Freddie Mercury...and, of course, Oscar Wilde, Walt Whitman, and John Waters. The latter was standing beside the gender-bending star Divine, dwarfed by the actor's bulk, a happy smile beneath his trademark pencil moustache.

The voiceover went on, "But—as is so often the case in this beautiful, shabby little world of ours—some people just can't let things be, and accept others for what they are. Some people can't mind their own fucking business, can they?"

Now Waters was onscreen, shaking his head and tutting censoriously; now Wilde, sitting in the lotus position.

He said, "Many theories have been propounded as to what causes homophobia in men; because, shamefully, it usually is men. Some blame religion, with its Biblical commands that 'thou shalt not lie with another man, nor listen to bad disco music and have excellent fashion sense.' Others blame patriarchal power structures, which rule the masses by creating division between man and fellow man, as well as man and woman."

More footage of famous gay men and women followed, Wilde's voice rolling over the top: "Still others believe that popular culture is the root cause, with its relentless advocacy of the nuclear family, its archetypal boy-meets-girl motifs. A psychologist might argue that homophobia is the manifestation of the subject's own latent homosexuality in a destructive manner. Whew—that's pretty heavy. And a few—the more unimaginative ones—fall back on the familiar, and blame the parents."

It cut to grainy home video of a father urging his toddler to run with a football, then back to Wilde, still in the lotus position.

"Personally, I think it's because most men are weak and

spineless and terrified of what their Neanderthal peers might think of them. But hey, what am I thinking…!" He slapped his forehead, a cartoonish gesture. "Why not ask someone who knows? Someone…at the coalface, as it were."

Wilde leaped up and went toward a door which opened onto a large, bare room, brighter than the murky hallways. The camera panned to the far corner, where Tommy was strung up like Jesus on a rudimentary cross, naked, tied to the wood by his wrists and ankles. His face had been painted garishly, like a bad imitation of a drag queen, his curly hair scraped into tiny pigtails. A feather boa was draped over his shoulders. He looked tired and scared but defiant, a sullen curl on his lower lip.

Wilde said cheerily, "Folks, a big hand, please, for Tommy, our pupil for the day. Say hello to the folks at home, Tommy."

Tommy mumbled, "Yeah, yeah. Fuck you. How's that?"

"Fuck me? Hmm. I believe it's the fact that you've got a serious problem with fucking another man that's gotten you here in the first place, Tommy."

The camera zoomed in on Tommy's face, blurred, then tweaked into proper focus. Wilde said, "As you can see, we've tried to broaden Tommy's horizons by introducing him to the fun—the sheer *liberation*—of wearing make-up. Think David Bowie in his heyday. Think Alex in *A Clockwork Orange*. Think Marilyn Manson, think New Romantic, think the Scarlet Pimpernel. *Think*, Tommy."

The footage cut to a profile view of Tommy and Wilde facing each other. Wilde said, "Now. I'll ask this once. It's a very simple question. Why do you beat up gay men?"

"I'm not saying shit to you, fag."

"Whitman. A little persuasion is needed here."

Whitman stepped forward and drove a large knife through Tommy's feet, sticking them to the wood. The handle vibrated slightly as Tommy screamed in agony and disbelief.

"Okay! Okay! Christ! Stop. Don't do that… Stop. You're

fucking crazy. I'll talk."

"Better. Now, once more: why do you beat up gay men?" Wilde asked. "And please, *please* have a good reason for this, Tommy."

The bound man shook his head. "I don't... Shit. I don't fucking know. It's just a bit of fun, man. Just a bit of fun."

"A bit of fun. So what you did to that guy tonight—the man at the club—knocking his teeth out—that was 'just a bit of fun.' Correct?"

"Got it in one. Just kicking around, man. You gotta take it out on someone, right? Might as well be a buncha disgusting faggots. I mean, come on. It's not like this is some kinda radical fuckin' view here, right? Most folks I know think the same way about those cocksuckers. Least I got the balls to do something about it..."

Wilde raised a finger to hush him, and looked at the ground in thought. Tommy closed his eyes; his head lolled down around his chest.

Wilde said, "Hmm. Yes. I think your case might prove to be a more involved one than we had hoped, Tommy. Drastic measures may be required to cure this patient."

Cut to Wilde addressing the camera, as a plainly terrified Tommy was lifted off the cross in the background, blood gurgling from the wound in his feet. Wilde smiled benevolently.

"Once again, we must reluctantly take our leave, folks. I hope you've enjoyed watching, and I know we have your prayers and best intentions as we face into the onerous task of revealing the error of his ways to Tommy. Poor, mindless little Tommy. You'd almost have to love him if he wasn't so utterly repellent."

More old footage: ceremonial religious processions from the Vatican, still photo selections from Robert Mapplethorpe's oeuvre, David Bowie in his glam rock years, that alien beauty and angular style.

Wilde said, in voiceover, "Anyway, as with our previous

subjects, the way will be long and hard, but the rewards are... Well. The rewards are self-evident. And you can rely on the Enforced Karma Clinic to use every power in our means to smooth that path."

Then he was there in close-up, twirling a large syringe in one hand, the point of the needle against his gloved index finger.

"You know, some people say that laughter is the best medicine. We find other methods work faster." He winked. "Stay watching."

It faded to black, with the words, "Karma TV—it could be YOU" surfacing on the screen, throbbing brightly, then dissipating, dissolving, a ghostly echo ebbing away into nothingness.

2008

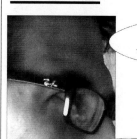

'No, I was just there, in the queue. You know, waiting for a teller to come open.'

'Alright, go on.'

'So these two idiots, I could hear them behind me. Two fat-necked fucking frat boys, right? You know the type. All bulked up. That irritating air of confidence they have. One of them's in my Modern History class, if you can believe that.'

'Uh-huh. You want another beer?'

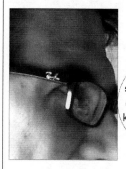

'Nah, I'm good with this one. So anyway, one of them was going on about... and he was talking really loudly, too. They always speak so that everyone can hear them. Anyway, he was obviously talking about his girlfriend or whatever, but he kept saying, "My bitch this, my bitch that", like he thought he was Snoop Dogg or something. "Aw, yeah, I told my bitch she'd better secure that shit or I'd slap her."'

'Ha ha ha. You do the impersonation quite well, Rob.'

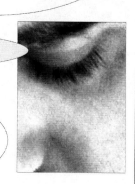

'I thank you. So dickhead number one is blah blah like that, and dickhead number two is snickering and then coming in with his own little comments. Like, uh, something like, "Yeah, man, the bitches gotta know who's boss", and so forth.'

'Uh-huh. ...You really do that impersonation well. It's funny.'

'Right, so anyhow, eventually I just couldn't, I'd had enough of listening to this horseshit. So I turned around and said, "Yeah, hey, couldn't help overhearing you there, sport. Talking about your bitch. Do you have a dog or something?" And he just looked at me like the fucking Neanderthal he was. Like, "Duuh?" So I said it again, "Do you have a dog? I hear you talking about your bitch, I wanna know do you keep a dog? 'Cause, uh, my brother, he's a pet doctor, he'd fix her right up for you, do a great job, if, you know, she gets sick or hit by a car or something."'

'You didn't... So what happened then? Did he even get the joke?'

'Oh, he got the joke. He got the joke, alright. Man, the guy looked fit to bust me wide open. Leaned in towards me, that big stupid frat-boy head right up close. "I oughtta pound your ass into the ground, you little faggot." Or some such witticism.'

'Oscar Wilde, watch out. ...Tch. What a dipshit. Pity Sandro wasn't there with you. Not that I'm, you know, I'm not saying you can't handle yourself...'

'No, you're right. Frat-boy outweighed me by, like, fifty pounds. Yeah, Sandro would have been good to have there. He'd have growled and this idiot would have shit his underwear. I wasn't too bothered, though. I mean, he wasn't gonna beat me up in a bank, was he?'

'No, I... Shit, it's annoying, though, isn't it? All that... It's not annoying. It makes me *angry*, Rob. I just think of Marie, or my mom, or Lillian... or any of your sisters, you know? Any of our friends. And these fucking guys, they... Makes me wanna...'

'Yeah, I hear ya, man. Makes you wanna break something, right? Or some*one*, ha ha. Hand me over that pack of cigarettes, would you?'

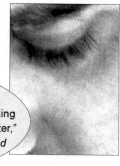

'I passed a tattoo parlor yesterday, you know that place next to the falafel place, and I swear, I half-thought about getting one. A big fucking tattoo, right across my chest: "He-Man Woman-Hater," like that song. Which, you know, is both ironic *and* snappy, so I obviously love it.'

'Don't bother. The mass of morons wouldn't get the irony. You gotta be blunt with some people. Hammer home the message.'

'I suppose so... Yeah, I think you're right. Shock tactics. A loud, sharp noise. A public spectacle. That'd command attention. ..."True terror is a language and a vision."'

'What's that?'

'Ah...something I read. Nah, you're absolutely right, Rob. Hammer it home.'

'Needs must when the devil drives, dude. And I don't even have any religion, but I'm pretty sure the devil is driving this motherfucker.'

Chapter 5

Stumped

THE light reduced to a microscopic point, then died completely, as Danny switched off the television set in his office and flopped back into a swivel chair. He kneaded his eyes and stretched his back. He stared dully at the screen and shook his head. The comforting patterns to be found in mundane actions. He smiled wryly and silently accused himself of subterfuge: this wasn't a pattern, it was a delaying tactic.

He had nothing, really. No leads, no useable physical evidence, no known felons who fit the profile. The gang was good, he had to concede: Rosenberg's sweep of the yuppie's apartment had yielded little beyond common fibers that could have come off any mass-retailed clothes. No prints on the videotape or the "courier" envelope. The voices, maybe—tie them down with voiceprint recognition—but that was more advantageous in proving guilt, not detecting the perpetrator. Besides, he was pretty sure the gang had doctored their voices. And more than that: after two confirmed abductions, he had no clues as to where all of it was leading. Danny hadn't come across something like this before: what were they, exactly? A bunch of pissed-off crazies on a mindless spree? No—there was purpose to what they were doing. Then what? A surrealist prank that had gone too far? Some sort of "New Men" in Rambo's clothing? But that was a ridiculous notion.

Or perhaps they were just personal enemies of that asshole Hudson? Ha. There was a definite possibility.

Danny stood and moved to the window, opening it a little to let the breeze in. He was surprised, and frustrated, at himself, because he was normally very good at figuring these things out. He was clever, he knew, and thoughtful, and remorselessly logical; and even the weirdest situations didn't normally throw him. He looked at the traffic sluggishly making its way along 35th Street, and thought about some of the odder cases he'd handled in nine years as a detective. There was one, from five or six years back, that he remembered particularly vividly: the victim of attempted murder who'd presented himself with stab wounds all over his back, places nobody could reach themselves, and declared that he had bludgeoned his wife to death in self-defense. She'd flipped, attacked him with the kitchen knife— what else could he do?

Danny didn't recall why he hadn't believed the guy's story— some unknowable instinct, some sense beyond the senses—but he'd checked it out anyway, poked around, followed the evidence like a beagle on a trail. Eventually he discovered that the supposed victim had rigged up an elaborate system of pulleys to inflict the wounds himself, as part of a cuckold's revenge. Danny had to admire his ingenuity, but didn't let that stop him nailing the vicious fuck.

A young, dull-looking officer burst in the door, his chubby face flush with excitement. Danny closed the window and said, "You don't know how to knock, no?"

"Sorry, sir. Dispatch said you'd wanna hear this right away. They've found a guy who might be, uh..." He cocked a finger at the video recorder. "...*your* guy."

Danny grabbed his jacket and checked that his pistol was secure in its shoulder holster. "Found where?"

"Chelsea, sir. Down by the water. He was..." The officer squinted at a piece of paper; it made his features even more porcine. "Right, he was strapped to a pier."

"Uh-huh. Anything else?"

The officer followed as Danny exited the room briskly. He gazed at the paper again and said, "Uh, lemme see. That area, sir, Chelsea, around Eighth Avenue, it's, uh... Well, it's, like, a major gay district."

Danny said, annoyed, "I know, Officer. Anything *else*?"

"Yes, sir. Victim, a young black male, was found naked, tied by his ankles, and bound hand and foot with..."

"...heavy duct tape. Is he alive or dead?"

"Still breathing, sir, but only just. They've jammed him on

over to Beth Israel. Suspected hypothermia from prolonged exposure. He musta been there for most of the night. Got a number of deep cuts, too: on the feet, the hands..."

Danny stopped abruptly. "Right. He's in the hospital. Fuck."

He punched the wall—not hard, but enough to startle the officer. The kid continued, "Uh, there was one other thing, sir. This guy, he had a whaddya call it, a placard hung around his neck. There was, uh, writing on it."

"What did it say?"

"Um, I'm not too sure what this means, but... 'How can they see the love in our eyes and still they don't believe us?' What is that? A line off a movie or something?"

Danny smiled, the cerebral wheels turning automatically. "It's... familiar to me. What is it...?" He touched his temple, thinking, then clicked his fingers and quietly hummed a tune for a few seconds. "Yes. It's from a song. *The Boy with the Thorn in His Side*, by The Smiths. English band. Good song. I used to like them in college."

"Uh...yes, sir. Is, uh, is that everything you need to know?"

"No. Call Beth Israel and ask them how soon this guy will be fit for questioning." The officer stood there dumbly. Danny waved his fingers. "Go on. Chop chop."

"Yes, sir."

Danny dialed a number into his cell phone as the kid trundled down the hallway.

"Cathy Morrissey, please. ...Hi, Cathy? Danny Everard. Cathy, what time did you receive that tape this morning? It was there when Bailey arrived for work. Which is...? And neither of you looked at it, you just sent it over here? ...Okay. Listen, Cathy, I'm gonna need to talk with you again today. What time would be...?" He checked his watch. "It's 10.30 now. Say 11? ...11.15. Okay, see you then."

He hung up as the officer returned, florid, gasping for breath. Danny had to commend him on his enthusiasm.

"Not a chance, sir. He's recovering, but he's too weak right now, and they can't get a word of sense outta him. They said call later. They said *maybe* this evening."

Danny nodded. "Right. Thanks, Officer."

A light drizzle began to fall as he swung his car around a bend in Chinatown. Danny was taking a roundabout way to the Network 4 offices; he wanted time alone, time to think about all of this. He felt, in one sense, that he was only reacting as yet, not acting. The case had no shape to it, no discernible outlines. But then he banished the thought as pointless: wasn't that how it was with most things? You just drift along, responding as best you can to events as they unfurl, hoping that nothing catastrophic awaits. And there were always things you could do, small things, but potentially significant. Danny reached for his phone and called the station.

"This is Detective Sergeant Everard. There's a videotape in the player in my office, and another sitting on top of the machine. I need them sent to forensics. I want to try and trace the voices on the tapes. The guys in balaclavas. I'm guessing they're disguised, but... Ask 'em to do what they can, alright?"

He disconnected just before the phone rang. Danny pressed the speaker button and Harte's deep bass voice rang out.

"Danny? James."

"Oh captain, my captain. What's up, James?"

"Just checking on progress. I called to your office but you'd already left. Would you believe I know the father of one of those boys you rescued yesterday? He's in my golf club."

"Well, I didn't quite rescue him. Which one?"

"Paul Hudson. Son's called Clint or Clifton or..."

"Clifford. I don't think he liked me very much."

"Well, if he's anything like the old man, he's an insufferable prick."

Danny laughed. "Yep, I'd say there's a certain genetic resemblance."

"Anyway, this moron is down my neck over the kid, so I need something to tell him. What have you got so far?"

Danny shrugged, and wondered why we often employ physical gestures that our conversational partner can't see. "Not a whole bunch, James. They're smart and resourceful and…and I hate to admit it, but they intrigue me."

"That's it? All I can tell this man is that the criminals who assaulted his son are of some academic interest to the investigating officer? Aw, no, Danny, please. Give me something more."

Danny eased the car to a halt at a red light. He looked through the rain at the busyness, the chaotic cadences, at the heart of Chinatown. Then he said, "They're dangerous. Tell your friend to count his blessings that his shitty son is still alive. And James— tell him I'm going to catch them."

He switched off the phone. "I hope."

Cathy smiled as Danny took a sip of the network's notoriously foul coffee, and laughed as he visibly winced at the taste.

She said, "Disgusting, isn't it? See, we're all used to it by now. You're still a virgin."

Danny laughed himself and said, "I've had worse. So tell me, where's the great Mr. Bailey today?"

"He's gone home. He said to apologize, but his famous ulcer is playing up, and anyway, he wouldn't be much help. He knows even less than I do, which is pretty much nothing."

"Guess we'll just have to muddle along as best we can." He arranged his notebook on the table at a slight angle to his body, and readied his pen. "Alright, run through a few details with me: the courier arrived at…?"

"Uh-uh. Wasn't a courier. It was posted."

Danny looked up in surprise. "Eh?"

"It was posted. Must have been either the final mail of last night or the first of this morning, because it was here when

Jonathon arrived."

He said, almost to himself, "I suppose...last post at ten... Sorry, I'm just trying to work out a chronology here. No return address, I presume?"

"Nope. We kept the envelope after our courier brought the tape over to you, if you want to check for yourself..."

Cathy leaned back and grabbed a thick padded envelope from a countertop, placing it on the table.

Danny took it and said, "Yeah...it's evidence, anyway. And that's it? Still no follow-up? No phone call, e-mail, anything?"

"I'm sorry. That's it."

Danny chewed on his lower lip and stared into space, a not-unattractive frown on his face. Cathy smiled inwardly—this odd situation was not entirely without its benefits. Her enjoyment of the view was interrupted when Patrick stepped into the room, blustering, "Cathy, could you...? Oh. 'Scuse me. I didn't know you had someone with you."

"No, no, it's okay," she said. "Come on in. You were there too."

Danny turned and stood, smoothing the creases in his jacket. Patrick stretched out his hand and said, "Aah—you must be Detective Everard. You're investigating the mysterious 3W case."

"Danny Everard. Pleased to meet you."

Cathy made a sweeping gesture and said, "Danny, this is Patrick Broder. He works in my department. He watched the first video with us."

"Everard," Patrick said. "That's an unusual name. Scottish?"

Danny smiled. "Actually, I think it's Irish. I'm a bit sketchy on the old family tree."

"How about that, Cathy? Another Irish person for you to go— what was it?— 'drinking and carousing' with."

"We're taking over the world, kiddo," she said. "Didn't I tell you?"

Patrick pulled up a stool. Danny resumed his seat, saying,

"So, Patrick—you've seen the first video as well?"

"Yeah. I don't know that I can tell you anything more than Cathy, though. I mean, it was weird, you know?"

Danny nodded.

"So what happened with those two guys?" Patrick asked. "The ones on the tape. They were found, right?"

"Yeah, we found 'em yesterday morning. They were fine. A bit shook-up. Actually, very shook-up. But they'll live."

"Well, that's good to know."

Danny smiled and stood, folding his notebook closed. "Yeah, I suppose it is. ...Listen, I'm gonna come clean here—I'm a bit stumped on this one. If either of you can think of anything— regardless of how insignificant it might seem—let me know straight away. Okay? Anything at all." He opened the notebook and scribbled on a page. "I'm gonna leave my direct line at the station and my cell number; you should be able to get me at one or the other."

He tore out the page and flattened it to the table. Cathy and Patrick stood, and all three exchanged handshakes.

Cathy said, "Of course, Danny. If we think of anything."

"Yeah. Whatever we can do to help, you know?" Patrick said. "And it was nice to have met you, Detective."

"Danny. Nice to meet you, too."

"Let me walk you down, Danny," Cathy said.

The detective moved outside; Cathy stopped and whispered back, "Call me a little crazy, but was he *flirting* with you just then?"

Patrick smiled and shrugged. "Hey, I can't blame the guy. It's my animal magnetism, Cath. It's irresistible."

She thumped him on the arm and followed Danny outside. He was about ten feet ahead, stopped, waiting for her. She trotted toward him and they began walking to the elevator.

Danny flicked his head back in the direction of Cathy's office and said, "Seems like a nice fellow."

"Who, Patrick? Yeah, he's sweet. He's just a boy, but he's sweet."

They had reached the elevator. Danny took a deep breath and turned to her, fixing Cathy in his gaze. She met his eyes and thought, Yep—I could answer your questions all day, Detective Danny Everard.

He said, "Listen, Cathy, I need you to keep a lid on all of this. I know this is a big story—I couldn't blame you for wanting to get the jump on your competition—but I need some time here. Just to get a proper handle on the situation. It's a bit crazy just yet. Can you do that for me?"

He made a silly, pleading sort of face, which didn't seem to suit him at all, and Cathy had to stop herself smiling. She liked Danny, she decided; he had good intentions and an inherent integrity. And he seemed oddly nervous just then, which endeared him to her even more.

She clasped his arm and said, "Sure, Danny. You can trust me."

"Appreciate it. We'll talk later, okay?"

He stepped into the elevator. Cathy stood there for a moment, a tiny smile playing on her lips, as the lights above the chrome doors marked his descent.

"Later. Okay."

The rain had stopped but a heavy bank of lead-gray clouds hovered ominously on the horizon. Danny was trotting down the steps of the Network 4 studio, a fresh wind tickling a chill along his neck, when another man sidled alongside and began walking in step with him.

"Detective Sergeant Everard? Daniel Everard?"

Danny stopped and warily examined him. The man was heavy, no taller than five six, his shiny hair brushed flat against his head. He wore a beige trench-coat and Danny thought, God, you are such a cliché. Might as well wear a fedora with "Scoop" written on the hatband.

The man introduced himself: "Leonard Krige, WRD News. You know, the cable channel? If I could just have a moment of your time, Detective…"

Danny started walking again, quicker now. Krige followed with a tape recorder held out before him. He called into the wind, "Just a quick moment, sir. It's about the so-called 3W Gang. Is it true that two nights ago, the sons of two well-known and influential New York bankers were tortured and left for dead in their own apartment?"

Danny stopped a second time and looked at Krige, incredulous. He shook his head contemptuously and walked off.

Krige, persistent, resumed his pursuit, saying, "And is it true that a second, related incident occurred last night, in which a young man was kidnapped and strung up naked near one of the city's most notorious homosexual districts?"

Danny stood and spoke without turning around. "Who told you that?"

Krige smiled triumphantly. "So it *is* true. Can I get an official comment, Detective?"

Danny muttered, "Get fucked, Krige" and started to jog down the rest of the steps. Krige shouted in his slipstream, "Hey, thanks a bunch. Shall I quote you on that?"

"Aw, *shit*. Shit, shit, shit."

Cathy closed her eyes and tapped the TV remote control unit off her forehead. Patrick shifted uncomfortably on the low leather couch in one of the station's screening rooms, feeling bad for her but at a loss as to how he could help. Cathy deftly removed her glasses and massaged her eyes with the same hand, then started flicking back up through the channels. It was obvious to both of them: all their rivals were on the scent of a scoop.

She stopped on a rolling newscast going out on a rival channel. The newscaster, a thin man of Indian descent, was saying, "...identity of the first two victims has been confirmed as Mr. Clifford Hudson and Mr. Steven Ainsworth, futures traders with the same Wall Street stockbrokers, although further details are not, as yet, available from official sources..."

An angry man with a large, handsome face came on screen as a mousy woman, presumably his wife, looked on in the background. Text underneath read, "Paul Hudson—father of victim." He bellowed into the small cluster of microphones before him, "It's been a full 36 hours since my son was discovered and *still* nobody has been arrested for questioning, nobody has been charged with any crime. The NYPD is acting like this is some sort of normal occurrence when anyone with a brain in their head can see that Clifford and Steven Ainsworth were the victims of a calculated attack by a well-organized..."

Cathy flicked again—Leonard Krige was reporting to camera, from the steps right outside her building. She wondered how much it'd hurt if she dropped a coffee-pot on his head from this height.

Krige said, "...off-the-record sources have confirmed to me that this incident is now being linked to the discovery this morning of an unconscious, naked man, tied to a pier in Chelsea. We can also confirm that Network 4 anchorman, Jonathon Bailey, was the recipient of two videotapes, purporting to come from the gang in question, which allegedly contain *actual* footage of these grisly attac..."

She muted the sound and sighed heavily. Patrick stood and took a step toward her, then realized that he didn't really know what to do. He sat down again.

Cathy said, "Jesus. This is...a disaster. I promised Danny. I *told* him it wouldn't get out, and now..." She pointed at the screen. "Look."

"It's hardly your fault, Cath."

"Whose fault do you think it is? I didn't leak any of this, but it was my responsibility. God *damn* it."

"Well…is there any way we can find out who's behind it? Who leaked the information?"

"No. Not really. It could have been anyone, Patrick. A member of staff, or the family of a member of staff, or someone who overheard something in a bar last night. I mean, it could have been *you*, for God's sake." Her cell phone rang, the love theme from *The Godfather* rendered in thin, electronic tones. "Hello? Yeah…uh-huh…the main boardroom. Got it. I'm on my way." Cathy pocketed the phone. "Fucking management—melodramatic to the last. I now have to travel upstairs and 'explain myself', quote-unquote, to the entire board of directors. Hold on a while here, will you? I'm pretty sure I'll feel like a drink in about 30 minutes."

"'Course I will."

She tutted quietly and left. Patrick settled into the soft couch and brought the sound back up on the television. Leonard Krige was just wrapping up on screen.

"Although we've already had one denial from the chief investigating officer, Todd, there seems little doubt that these two bizarre incidents are, indeed, linked. What happens next is anyone's guess, but the feeling I've been getting from sources is that something definitely *will* happen: sooner or later. This is Leonard Krige…" He gave that fake, practised news media smirk. "…for once, at the Network 4 studios."

Patrick killed the set. He sat there momentarily, absently pulling at a small tear in the couch's fabric. He pictured Cathy, right now, entering the boardroom, a row of unsmiling faces in suits ranked around the table, a wall against which her wave could break. He sighed, and reached for his phone. Not much he could do about it at the moment, anyway. They'd all have to wait, he figured, and allow things to take their course.

NEW YORK HERALD-CHRONICLE   SATURDAY, AUGUST 11TH

Outrage at Mosque 'Desecration'

by REBECCA HANDLER

OUTRAGE has 'been expressed by Muslim community leaders and church elders at what they describe as the 'desecration' of a Manhattan mosque. And Ibrāhīm al-Turābī (54), outspoken imam at the East 12th Street Mosque, has called on police to take immediate action against a 'blatantly racist and anti-Muslim outrage'.

Local police have confirmed that a bizarre mural was painted onto the wall of the mosque's room for prayer. It apparently depicted Allah, wearing a long dress and ballroom dancing with a man of Asian ethnicity. Flowers and ribbons are strewn around their heads, and at their feet a scroll reads, 'Try a little tenderness…' It is against Islamic belief to pictorially represent Allah.

One police source revealed, 'The thing was done with, we think, a very large stencil of some kind and spray-paint in a can. It's pretty much the one color, just a sort of outline, a silhouette. But it's pretty clear.'

When asked how churchgoers could be sure the figure in the dress represented Allah, the same source replied: 'Simple – the name-tag pinned to his dress.'

Ibrāhīm al-Turābī became embroiled in controversy last month when he delivered a passionate defence of church member, Hassan Ali Jinnah (46), who had been convicted of murder following the so-called 'honor killing' of his daughter, Irshad (19).

Mr. Ali Jinnah said in court that his daughter had 'disgraced her family, her faith and her people' by having a child with her boyfriend, a local man of Chinese parentage.

Mr. al-Turābī subsequently denounced the life sentence from the steps of his mosque, declaring, 'This man did only what any loving father would do. Perhaps if this society cannot respect the rightness of our actions, we should not respect this society.' Many prominent politicians reacted angrily to his comments.

The investigation continues.

Chapter 6

Playing poker

STREETLIGHTS were pricking into life outside as Danny walked through the hospital corridors, his long overcoat billowing behind him like a superhero's cape. The smell of antiseptic and something else, some cold, unpleasant odor, filled his nostrils. He paused to check directional signs, followed the arrow and stepped into an elevator that began to ascend.

Wilde, Waters, and Whitman sat around a low table in a basement uptown. Music played softly in the background— instrumental, evocative. Beer bottles, packs of cigarettes, and ashtrays littered the table. Waters started to deal out cards, their papery snap on the table's hard plastic top a steady counterpoint to the music.

Danny reached his floor, stepping out and walking down a long corridor. Large rectangular lights glowed overhead, reflected in the shining tiles on which he walked. A thin man in rimless round glasses stepped out of a door to Danny's right, shaking his hand.

"Doctor Ronald Troussier," he said softly. "I'm handling the patient for the time being."

"Detective Sergeant Danny Everard. 'For the time being.' What does that mean exactly? How serious is his condition?"

Troussier beckoned Danny to follow him into the tense hush of Tommy's room.

The basement was clean, with plain white walls and banks of electronic equipment on two sides: several computers and modems, a laser printer, a camera on a tripod and one on a shelf, a sound-editing desk, a radio scanner, stacks of CDs, movies on disc and cassette, a bulky, old-fashioned microfiche which gave that corner an air of retro kitsch. Cables snaked from machine to machine, to central power points and wall jacks. A huge banner, made of some sort of netting, was fixed to the four corners of the ceiling, sagging slightly in the centre. It said, "LA LUCHA

CONTINÚA" in thick, white letters, an old-style military typeface.

The hand had been dealt, and the three men examined their cards.

Whitman drawled, "Um...I bet 20."

"20? Don't be stupid," Waters responded. "You can't just bet 20. You gotta start with something decent. Like, say, 50."

"I told you, I'm a bit short this week. Had to get new tires for the bike. I'm fucking broke, man."

Wilde said, "I'll lend you the money, Sandro. Alright? Now can we please play the game, you collective pain in the ass? Thank you."

Danny and Troussier stood together, a few feet back from the intensive care unit in which Tommy lay, hooked up to different pieces of equipment: a drip, nasal prongs, a cardiac monitor, a chest drain to the left side. Danny actually shuddered—he was physically brave enough, but being around the weak and unwell touched a nerve of uneasiness, the sureness of his mortality. He thought about death a lot; he didn't fear it, but did recoil from it, instinctively. That immutable impulse to continue existing.

He said, "So? Gimme a situation report, or whatever you medical people say."

Troussier smiled. "Well, I suppose diagnosis is the most commonly used term. Alright: the patient suffered fairly serious hypothermia but is recovering reasonably well. He also had deep knife wounds on the feet, hands and, believe it or not, one under the left rib cage."

"The marks of the crucifixion. Jesus Christ."

"The very same, or so I've been told. However, those aren't what worry me right now. His wounds have been sutured, and we've repaired the tendon damage to both hands. He's also had a chest drain inserted for bleeding into the lung. In general, Detective, his physical condition is stable and he should recover from those injuries. But there's something else."

Various books lined the shelves: books on philosophy, psychology, gender, history, fiction. A diversity of subjects and writers, and an eclecticism in their arrangement: Simone de Beauvoir beside James Ellroy, Noam Chomsky nestling up to Alan Moore, *Fear of Flying* looking almost self-conscious next to *The Official Slacker Handbook*. The clip of a handgun, though, looked less incongruous, resting on a history of Ulrike Meinhof and the 1970s guerrilla campaign that she led.

Waters cleared his throat. He took a sip of beer and said, "Listen. Uh…I gotta say something."

Wilde said, distractedly, "Oh, yeah?"

"Yeah. It's, ah…it's about our friend. You know, from the other night?"

Wilde looked at him over the fan of his cards. "You can say his name, Rob. We're not bugged here. Tommy. You're talking about Tommy."

"Right. Tommy. I'm a bit… I think we might have gone too far the other night, okay?"

"Go on, doctor. What are you worried about?"

Troussier sighed, paused, formulating his words. He had worked with police before, and other non-medical people, and knew how easily the terminology of his profession could convert to meaningless white noise by the time it reached the listener's ears.

"The patient has been given something," he began. "Actually, two things. First off, a mild cocktail of sedatives and muscle relaxants—fairly harmless in the long term. He's probably gotten over that already. But also another drug, which is where I start to worry. It's hard to tell exactly what just yet—we're running tests—but I'd guess one of the psychoactive or hallucinogenic drugs. LSD, maybe, or mescaline. Damned if I know *why* this might have been done, but all the physiological and neurological signs are there." He smiled wryly. "This kid is fried."

Danny nodded, thinking, working to fit this information into its background context. He said, "A mood-altering drug. Great. This gets better and better. Okay: tell me what something like this does to a person. What reaction it causes."

"I was up there earlier. At the hospital," Waters said. "He looked...fucked up, man. Really bad."

Wilde leaned back and let his gaze drift over the walls, covered with home-made artwork, notes and reminders, scavenged advertizing placards and public works signs, and a myriad of posters: rock groups, sports stars, cultural icons, bikini pin-ups. Ali made shapes with those monumental fists and Laetitia Casta beamed, crazily sexy in a gold lamé swimsuit, her imperfect teeth just making her more attractive.

He said, "Of course. That's the whole point, isn't it?"

"No, you don't understand. I know what we're doing here. I know it's gotta hurt. But Tommy, man... He was at death's door, alright? And we'd put him there, and that is too fucking far."

They moved to the side of Tommy's bed, the doctor's head tilted in an attitude of concern.

He said, "Okay. It's complicated, alright—and I'm not being patronizing—but in layman's terms, hallucinogenic drugs work on the neurotransmitters in the brain: the information pathways. A lot depends of the user's state of mind at the time, and the surrounding environment, but basically, they can induce temporary symptoms of psychosis, cause visual and audio illusions, amplification of the senses, altered self-awareness...a whole heap of different effects. And a list of physical symptoms as long as the proverbial arm."

Danny grimaced. He badly needed a smoke.

"*Riiight*. I'd be lying if I said I understood all of that, but I get the general gist of it. They gave him something to bring on hallu-cinations, more than likely. Fuck with his head a little, anyway.

Still doesn't explain *why*, though. I mean, was it just some sort of punishment, or...?"

"We're not just thugs or vigilantes, Rob," Wilde said. "We don't just pass judgment and punish. We're making a stand and making a statement to the collective consciousness of a screwed-up, shitty society, and Tommy? What we did? That was his education, and everyone else's."

Across town Tommy's eyes flickered open, the barest glint of life in them. He was coming around, slowly. He stared dully at Danny and Troussier, still talking, their voices faint and faraway. He didn't know where he was or who they were. He just knew he was hurting but still alive.

Troussier was saying, "...to get this stuff? Well, it's supposed to be strictly regulated, but as I'm sure you're aware, 'supposed to' doesn't always mean it is. I don't know, Detective. On the internet, a street-dealer maybe, a contact in a hospital or pharmaceutical plant..."

Then Tommy began to remember—hazy snatches of memory picked from the ether. His mind left the room, the two men by his bed receding from his consciousness as he drifted back into the past—to the last thing he remembered...

Disorientation, unnerving dreaminess—pockets of memory bubbling to the surface of Tommy's mind. He was in that warehouse again, that empty, spooky place with its stained walls and metallic echoes. And those creeps in the hoods were strapping him into a chair and smoothly sliding a needle into his forearm. So sharp, he remembered, so sharp he didn't even feel the spike pierce his skin. The big one clasping Tommy's head tightly, hands like twin vices around his skull, while the smaller guy yanked his eyelids up and taped them into place, forcing him to look straight ahead at a screen. He struggled against the grip, even tried to bite their fingers. But there was no escape. Then paralysis settling slow, from heart to extremities, a weird leakage of energy; and weirder still, a feeling of indifference. He couldn't move and his brain was telling him that he didn't care. Then the man in the doctor's smock, leaning into his view and smiling. The fucker actually *smiled* at him.

"Ever seen *A Clockwork Orange*, Tommy? Not half as good as the book, really, but there was one good scene." Standing aside to reveal a video screen. "The Ludovico Technique, Mark II: take it away, men..."

The three men in the basement threw down cards, tipped long columns of ash from their cigarettes, hoisted their beer bottles. The game continued.

Waters said, "I'm scared. Not for myself, or that we're gonna get caught. I'm scared we'll go too far and someone will die. It's as simple as that."

"That won't happen, Rob," Wilde said. "Look at me. That's not gonna happen, okay? Everything will go as it should."

Whitman mulled over which card to drop and said, "Yeah, don't worry about it, buddy. It's all under control."

He punched Waters on the arm. Even though he was only playing, it still hurt.

The big guy didn't have to hold his head now; didn't have to force him. Tommy watched it all. A rolling montage of images cutting crazily from scene to scene: images of war and peace, love and violence, sex and death and inhumanity—some surreal, some frighteningly real. His mind was lifting from its moorings; something in his system now, something else in that needle. The pictures retreating and rebounding, bigger, smaller, stretched out of shape, the volume altering wildly. A buzz inside his ears, his eyes blurring, but not enough to block it out.

Marching soldiers at the Nuremberg Rallies; a man's head

exploding in a cheap horror movie; girls putting flowers into the gun barrels of Soviet tanks; red lips, in close-up, vivid and voluptuous, almost over-ripe; fires on a chemically polluted lake; riot police beating a man through his bloodied shirt; a bald, professorial type, eye bulging and distorted against the camera, laughing hysterically; a feral, shaven-headed soccer hooligan baring his teeth; a woman fleeing from an alleyway, her dress torn, panic on her face; the taut, muscular sculpture of a line of Mapplethorpe-style nudes, a homoerotic frieze.

Then a close-up of a boot kicking a man's face, over and over, in visceral, nauseating detail. Tommy swayed dizzily; the big man righted him, fixing his view on the screen again—where the face being kicked was morphing into his own. The real Tommy shrieked in fright, his feet scrabbling on the ground to get away from it. Panic like a blood-flow throughout his body.

The leader, the smart-talker, leaning across again, saying, "No further comment, I believe, is necessary."

Tommy had passed into unconsciousness before he found out what happened to the man with his face.

Wilde dropped his cards, breathed heavily, looked Waters in the eye.

"You trust me, right? You believe in what we're doing, don't you? Rob?"

"I... Yes. I'm worried, but I trust you."

"Look: we're doing the right thing, you guys. Believe me— people are starting to listen." He took a cigarette from the pack and passed it to Waters. "Soon they'll actually hear what we're saying."

Tommy was almost fully awake. He had returned to the present and now tried to speak, the words a faint whisper at first.

"Muh...muh...mother..."

Danny and Troussier continued their conversation, oblivious, until Tommy sat up sharply and hollered, "Mother*fuckers*! You goddamn motherfuckers!"

They rushed to him, easing him back onto the pillow. Troussier did whatever routine checks doctors did in these circumstances; Danny gripped Tommy's face.

"Can you hear me? Hey. Nod if you can hear me."

Troussier said, "Just a moment, Detective. I'd prefer if you allowed me to..."

"No. Look, you're the doctor, and in two minutes you can do whatever you need to do. But I need to know what this man knows right now. Please."

The doctor reluctantly nodded acquiescence and stepped back, a watchful eye on the scene.

Danny said, "Kid—can you hear me? Just nod."

Tommy nodded, weakly.

"Okay. Good. I'm gonna ask you a few questions," Danny said. "You don't have to speak. Just nod or shake your head. Do you understand that?"

Another nod.

"Alright. Did you recognize either the men who abducted you, or the place they brought you to?"

A shake of the head.

"Were their voices disguised?"

A nod for yes.

"And there's nothing you remember that could be used for identification? A license plate, a...a street-sign, a smell, a sound, anything?"

Tommy shook his head again.

"Alright," Danny said. "That's okay; I suppose I didn't expect anything. Look, you, ah, you get well soon, yeah?"

He had turned to leave when Tommy started whispering again—a low, insistent rustle. Danny leaned in close. The man seized his arm, incoherence and alarm in his eyes, and said, "W-why me, man? I didn't... Why me? I just kicked shit out of a few faggots, man. You...a cop. A tough guy. You understand, right?"

He slumped back onto the pillow again, exhausted. Danny looked at him for a long moment. He walked past Troussier toward the door, saying, "He's all yours. I think I should leave now. The atmosphere here; it, ah, it doesn't agree with me."

He paused at the door as Troussier replied: "You get used to it, Detective. You get used to it until it feels like normal."

NEW YORK HERALD-CHRONICLE   TUESDAY, AUGUST 21ST

Letters to the Edi

SIR – Alan Kouts writes in yesterday's letters page, 'I'm sick of being pushed around and told what to do by these tree-huggers and feminazis, not to mention the homosexual lobby who want to destroy the family. It's time to take the fight back to these malcontents. It's time for all us real men to engage in battle for the soul of this nation.'

As a tree-hugging feminazi of many years, I simply say: I couldn't agree more. Let battle begin.

Yours, etc.,

N R Graves

Chapter 7

Klub Khan

WHAT a ridiculous fucking name for a place like this: Klub Khan. Danny had drank here a few times, though not often, and every time he visited he couldn't help marveling at the stupidity of that name. Was it some sort of reference to Kublai Khan or Genghis Khan, he wondered? Did the proprietors believe guys like that would hang out in this sort of club? Doubtful. He lit a cigarette and it struck him that maybe this was an oblique tribute to that British band from the 1980s, Frankie Goes to Hollywood. Gay trailblazers, scandalous, iconic in their own way. They mentioned the younger Khan in one of their songs, didn't they?

But who cared, anyway? He crushed the cigarette underfoot, took a deep breath and stepped inside. The place wasn't as packed as normal, which was good, though they still had those unearthly strobe lights that usually gave him a headache. Danny didn't like clubs as a rule—he preferred a quiet, European-style bar, on his own, with a beer and the newspaper (and a packet of smokes before the accursed ban came in)—but this wasn't the worst joint in the world. And he had a reason for coming here, he rationalized, as music thudded in the background and a few guys half-heartedly danced under spinning disco balls. Clusters stood around talking and drinking. Danny scanned the place and sighed, then moved to the bar. He caught the bartender's attention.

"Hey. Uh, beer, please. Beck's if you have it."

He sipped his drink, watching the crowds so intently that he didn't notice a second man approaching.

"Good choice. Higher purity standards."

Danny looked at him, startled. "What?"

The man pointed at Danny's bottle. "German beer. They have higher purity standards in their brewing techniques. That's why they're so renowned for the quality of their beer. Not like the piss we make here. Hi—I'm Michael."

He held out a hand and smiled. Michael was big, very broad across the chest and shoulders—gym sculpted, Danny knew straight away, not the body of a manual worker. He wore his hair in a high quiff that made his head look oddly angular, but he was a good-looking guy.

Danny returned the shake and said, "Right. Higher standards. Well, that's very interesting, Michael."

"No it isn't, but it's nice of you to lie like that. So what do you think of the new design?"

"Design for...?"

"The club." Michael swept a hand across the room. "The new lights? The dancefloor? The seat coverings in the booths? It's all been changed recently."

"Right. Sorry, I, ah... I haven't been here in a while."

"I really like it. It's funky and modern, but the place has still got that cozy sort of homey feel to it, you know?"

Danny shrugged. "I...guess so. Sorry, are you in interior design or something?"

Michael gave a nice, unguarded laugh and said, "Ha! Me? God, no. You've got the right field, but not interior. Web design. I know, I know. It's all just a fad and the bottom's gonna fall out of the whole online phenomenon any day now and leave me jobless and penniless and what, oh *what*, will I do then? Been hearing that for 15 years."

Danny laughed also. "Aw, I dunno. You seem like a fairly resourceful character."

"Again, no, but thank you for lying like that. So what did you say your name was?"

"I didn't." Danny winced in embarrassment. "Sorry. That's such a cliché."

"Okay, I'll try and better that. 'Do you come here often? What's a nice nameless guy like you doing in a recently redesigned place like this?'"

They both laughed. Michael said, "So if I can't have your name, can I at least know what you do? You know, sort of balance things up between us?"

"I'm a policeman, Michael. A detective."

Michael nodded slowly, surprisingly impressed. "No shit. Well, good for you. I'll know who to call the next time I get mugged while hailing a cab. Except I won't, right, because I don't know your name?"

They laughed again. Neither spoke for a few moments. Faster music was pulsing over the sound system now. Danny stared at the glossy countertop and suddenly felt very tired. It had been a waste of time coming here.

Then Michael said, "*Anywaayy*... I don't believe in standing on ceremony with these things, so I'll just come straight out with it: I think I like you. And I think I'd like to go somewhere else with you."

Danny rubbed his eyes and took a drink. He said, "Ah...listen, Michael. You seem like a really nice guy—sincerely—but I've just had a tough few days and a worse fucking break-up, and all I really wanna do is stand here and get slowly, horribly drunk. Is that okay? I don't want you to be upset or anything."

Michael smiled and moved to leave. "Nah. Nah, that's cool. Another time, maybe."

"You never know."

"Take care, Mister Policeman."

Danny called another beer and looked around some more, looked at the couples smooching on the dancefloor and two men in red suspenders having an intense discussion at their table. Maybe they're discussing whether to finally leave the 1980s and ditch the suspenders, Danny thought. He moved onto whiskies, letting the alcohol seep into his system, feeling it loosen out the knots, that warm, careless glow radiating from his head to his limbs. This is why people drink, he decided: it didn't make you forget, it just made you not give a shit.

He was about to leave when he spotted Peter crossing the floor. Danny rushed across and grabbed him, whirling him around. Peter eyed him warily.

Danny said, "Peter! I'm so glad to see you here. I thought you might be here, I didn't know, but I figured..."

"Danny, stop it. What...what is this? What do you want from me?"

"What do I...? Jesus, I wanna *talk* to you, Peter. I wanna explain, about what happened and all that stuff I said. Did you get my messages? Phone and e-mail."

Peter sighed angrily and rubbed his temples. He was small, verging on tiny, and very smartly dressed, with designer geeky glasses and a thin strip of goatee beard on his chin. He stood next to a huge man in a sleeveless muscle top and tapered-leg denims. They looked mismatched. The big guy glowered at Danny and seemed like he was about to step in when Peter raised a hand.

He said, "It's alright, François. Just...go back to the table. Actually, get our coats, will you? I'll meet you outside in a minute."

François eyeballed Danny before moving off. Danny said, "Whoa. Wait. You're leaving? You can't. We have to talk, dammit."

He laid his hand on Peter's arm, who threw it off angrily. "We have *nothing* to talk about. Got that, Danny? Nothing. And there *is* nothing between us; not any more. Now please piss off and leave me alone. You're causing a scene."

"Peter, what...? Man, think, will you? Think about us, and what you're doing. Come home, Peter. Please. We can work this out if you'll only fucking *talk* to me!"

Peter closed his eyes tight, then looked at Danny. "Okay, Danny. Fine. We'll talk. Alright? But not here. Call me tomorrow around noon. We can get some lunch and... I don't know. See what we can do about this. Is that satisfactory?"

"Well...no, not really. For God's sake, Peter, we need to sort this out. I'm only asking for five minutes here..."

Peter brushed past him and began walking to the front door. He called back, "Leave it, Danny. Call me tomorrow when you're sober."

"Fuck you, I am not fucking *drunk*!"

Peter walked quickly toward the entrance, sprinting almost. Danny went after him, stumbling a little, distraught and more inebriated than he had realized. As the door closed behind Peter, shutting him off from view, Danny bumped into another man, a thick-necked youngster in a shiny shirt, making him spill his drink.

The guy looked down at the spreading stain, indignant, and said, "Look what you just did to my shirt, you asshole. My fucking DKNY shirt."

"Listen, man, I'm sorry. I'm in a hurry."

The man placed a bejeweled hand on Danny's chest. "You're in a hurry, huh? Well, that's fine. That more than makes amends for my ruined fucking shirt, doesn't it?"

"Look—I said I was sorry, okay? It was an accident. Now move out of my fucking way, please."

"Do you know how much this shirt cost, you dipshit? Probably more than you earn in…"

Danny shoved him aside. The man said, "You clumsy, drunken, stupid son of a bitch" and threw a wild punch, scuffing Danny on the side of the head. He snapped then, slamming the guy to the wall and punching him several times in the head, enjoying it and repenting it all at once. Two security men rushed him, beefy giants in tight black t-shirts and earpieces, tearing him off the other man and wrestling him to the door.

Danny kicked and struggled, shouting over his shoulder, "How's your DKNY shirt now, pal? *Huh*!? Matches your fucking *face* now!"

They hurled him out and he fell to the ground, crouching there, one knee in a puddle. He said quietly, "God…damn…it. Idiot. *Idiot*."

Across the street Peter and his new beau were slamming the doors on their car. Peter stared straight ahead as François gunned the engine. The osmosis of the puddle water moved up Danny's trouser leg, that cold crawl. He was feeling thoroughly miserable for himself when his phone rang.

He fumbled for it, pressing the connect button as he stood up: "Danny Everard... What? Can you speak up, there's a lot of background noise here... Okay, slow down: two or three men in balaclavas...unmarked white van...yeah, that sounds like my guys. Gimme an address... Brooklyn. Seen driving toward Red Hook..." He began walking briskly to his car, parked on an adjacent street. "Alright, put out an APB with all available units in that area. Have them cruise within a ten-block radius of where the pimp was snatched and give a description of everyone involved. It's not much to go on, but... I'm on my way there now. And listen: contact me *immediately* you hear anything, got me? That means right fucking away."

Danny sprinted to his car, wrenched the door open and hesitated for a moment—he was definitely over the legal limit, but was he safe to drive? He screwed his eyes shut and tried to slow his heartbeat. Got to work out the balance, Everard. Weigh the risk against a greater danger.

Fuck it. He shook his head rapidly, like a dog emerging from a swim, gritted his teeth, climbed in, and turned the key.

Blackness. Whispers flitting from left to right like bats through night-time treetops.

"I still think it was a bad idea to just do it like that. Right off of the street."

"Yeah, that was risky, man. In plain sight like that...anyone could have gotten a mark on us, you know?"

"Exactly. The van, the direction we were going... I gotta say, I don't like this."

"Relax, guys. I told you, we needed to make a more...dramatic statement. Something bold and witty. To snatch someone off the street, like a daring costumed hero." Laughter.

"Anyway, it's all okay. The van's unmarked, right? We drove in a circle to get here. The whole thing only took about five seconds, and the only witnesses were winos or crack-addicts; neither renowned for their powers of observation. And besides which: why would *anyone* care if a piece of shit like this goes missing?"

The blindfold was ripped off, and Painter blinked into the glare of a spotlight, set up on a stand about 20 feet away. He looked down and back up, and there were three men in tuxedos and masks, their eyes dark and watchful behind black wool. Three little bastards in fancy suits. They were in an enormous, empty room in an even more enormous, empty warehouse complex. Painter looked down again: he was tied to a wooden chair, stripped to his underpants and vest.

Wilde, standing in the center of the three, said, "Painter. That's what they call you, right? 'On the street.' Or whatever stupid fucking terminology you people use."

Painter gazed slowly around the room, then smiled at Wilde. He was heavyset, in his mid-forties, with a moustache and broad Latino features. He was also scarred, leathery, and mean.

He said, "Yeah, man. I paint pretty pictures, haven't you heard? I could do a fine job on this place you got here. It needs some pretty pictures."

"Ah. A comedian, too," Wilde said.

"Isn't everyone these days, Wilde?"

"Too true, Waters. All too true. Right: start the camera."

Painter's craggy face, staring at the ground, popped up on the viewfinder as Waters focused in properly, the whirr of the camera a low background note.

Wilde said, "So why do they call you 'Painter', then, Painter?"

The pimp smiled and looked away, shaking his head.

"Ho-hum. Another reticent interviewee. Whitman, a little persuasion again, please."

Whitman took two large steps and slammed his hunting knife into the chair, millimeters from Painter's groin. He gasped and jumped back.

"Obviously, I don't need to tell you that he deliberately missed," Wilde said. "Whitman could slice off that pathetic excuse you call a dick and have it sliced and stir-fried and fed to you with soy sauce before you felt the first cut, so don't fuck around with us. Why do they call you Painter?"

"Because I like my bitches to wear a lot of make-up," Painter sighed. "You know, get glamorous."

"And a fashion connoisseur as well. Aren't you the talented one?"

Waters said, "A regular renaissance man."

Painter shrugged. Wilde started to walk back and forth, slowly, hands behind his back. He said, "And how many—to use the argot of the working pimp—'bitches' do you run, Mr. Painter?"

"I d'nno. Twenny, twenny-one, twenny-two...it depends."

"On what?"

"Whether they're in jail or not. Whether they're using. Whether they've run off, or gone home to mama, or just ain't arrived on the fucking Greyhound yet. Man, why are you asking me this shit?"

"So if your girls are using drugs...what? They don't go to work?"

Painter laughed, rasping and jaded. "Ha! You stupid motherfucker. My ho's work for me if the fucking *veins* are hanging out of their skinny little arms, know what I'm sayin'? If they can persuade someone to fuck 'em, then they workin'."

Wilde considered this for a moment, then stepped forward and slapped Painter, hard, on the face. "I have a little problem with your language, Painter. The next time you use the words 'bitch', 'ho' or 'fuck' in its sexual sense, I'm going to stick your left hand to the chair with a screwdriver. Okay?"

"You gotta be..." The pimp bit down on his lip, corralling his anger. He had pride, but he also had survival instincts. "Yeah, sure, man. Okay, sure. You're the man in charge here."

The fog was clearing from Danny's head, finally. He'd driven across the Brooklyn Bridge with the window down and the cold night air had sliced through and around him, shook him up, slapped his face. He had also literally slapped his own face, more than once. He risked pulling into a drive-thru for a coffee, balancing it between his knees and taking hot, reviving sips as he trawled the area of Brooklyn the white van was seen heading in. He didn't feel too confident of passing a breathalyzer test any time soon, but reckoned he was alert enough to react to whatever Wilde and his pals might attempt next.

Danny drained the dregs of his coffee and tossed the cup onto the floor, guiltily half-hoping that he wouldn't have to put that theory to the test. He reached an intersection, cruising slow, and spotted a white van which roughly fit the description. He pulled to a halt and lightly touched his gun, and then two overweight men in their late thirties came into view, hoisting a sofa, struggling under its weight.

He rolled down the window and leaned out. "Hey! You two. NYPD. Step out where I can see you."

The workmen dropped the sofa and walked toward Danny's car with sheepish expressions. One held up his hands and said, "Hey, shit. I'm sorry, officer. We're gonna move it in two minutes. I know it's restricted parking, we're just dropping off some furniture. My sister's place. Two minutes, swear to God…"

"No, it's… You're fine. Carry on with what you're doing. Listen—you haven't seen another white van? In the last few minutes? Much the same as yours."

The same man shrugged. "Don't know. Could have, I guess. It's not really the type of thing you pay much attention to, you know?"

"No, I guess not. Alright. Thanks."

The men resumed their work, cautiously, a little apprehensive for no other reason than the fact that authority had that effect on some people. Danny had experienced it sometimes, even in social situations: that barely perceptible tautening in the face once someone found out he was a cop, the feeling that the other person was automatically censoring their words now, without even realizing they were doing it. He didn't feel bitter about it, he understood it, but it could play havoc with your sense of ease at a dinner party. Here comes a cop, hide the doobie. He'd done it himself as a kid.

Danny realized that his hand was still at his gun. He moved it and pulled the car away.

"Well, that's the background detail. Now let's get down to the nitty-gritty. Have you ever, say, killed one of your girls?"

Painter laughed, whorls of dense muscle tensing and releasing as his torso heaved. His body language screamed out that the laughter was fake. "What...? Man, that's funny. And you called *me* the comedian."

Wilde said flatly, "Answer the question, you scumbag."

The pimp glared at him. He was beginning to lose patience with these candy-ass motherfuckers and their dressing-up games. "I plead the Fifth. Alright? Ain't that my constitutional right?"

"I'm sorry. You seem to be laboring under the misapprehension that this is some sort of courtroom. Where your 'rights' automatically apply."

"Well, if this ain't a trial of some kind, what the fuck is it?"

Wilde picked at a piece of fluff on his lapel, off-white against the tuxedo's black. He looked up and said, "The start of your education, Painter. You're a lucky man—you get to go back to school when so many of your disenfranchised peers won't. Now answer me. Honestly."

Silence. Wilde glared down and Painter held the stare. No response. Wilde slapped his prisoner's face again, a dull crack that rebounded around the room's stripped walls.

"I said answer my fucking question!"

A few slaps on the face didn't faze a man like Painter. His back was tattooed with three bullet holes and his shoulder bore a six-inch machete scar. He smiled, purely out of stubbornness, to irritate this son of a bitch. He continued to eyeball Wilde, who slapped him again, harder and harder. Wilde could feel sweat beads pop up on his skin, under the balaclava, as a trickle of blood formed at the corner of Painter's mouth.

Wilde said, in breathy bursts, "You worthless fucking waste of oxygen. Tell me. I want to hear you say it. I want to hear you admit that you've raped and killed and used those women like pieces of meat. Tell me, goddammit!"

Then Painter snapped and sat up, shouting, "Yeah, I fucking killed a few! You happy now, you crazy bastard? I beat one to death with my golf club, and I let the other die of a fucking overdose! You like that, bastard? You *like that*!? And I'd do it again!" He paused, closed his eyes, breathing heavily through his broad nose. "I'll do whatever the fuck I want to whoever the fuck I want. Got me? A bitch is a bitch, be she fat, skinny, young or old. I take 'em from the cradle and I take 'em when they're nearly in the grave, and then I *put* 'em in the grave! So fuck them, and fuck *you*!!"

Wilde stepped back, squeezing the bridge of his nose. Whitman and Waters looked at each other. Wilde said, barely more than a whisper, "Get up."

Painter said, "What?"

"Get out of the chair. Whitman—cut him loose. Do it!"

The big man hesitated, trying to remember if this was part of the plan, then shrugged and dexterously slit Painter's binds.

Wilde said, "Give him his trousers."

Whitman threw the pimp's trousers at him. Painter pulled them on, suspicious, while Wilde untied his shoelaces.

"The law of the jungle, right?" Wilde said. "Survival of the fittest and all that? That's how it works in your world, isn't it?" He stood tall with his hands out and his feet bare. "Well, come on then, fucker. Show me how tough you are when a man is facing you. Come on!"

Painter hesitated, then lunged at Wilde who pushed him past, spinning lightly, his feet arching up from the toes. The other man charged again, low-centered, long arms, head down like a warring ape. His punches were blocked easily, almost tauntingly. This was brute violence against cool technique, and there was no contest. Wilde hit him a few times, powerful blows square on the face.

He said, "It's a hard fucking lesson, my man, but you're gonna learn it. What have you to say about your girls now?"

"I told you, whoreson: a bitch is nothin' but a bitch."

Wilde leaned back and struck out with a rigid leg, kicking Painter in the chest, driving him back.

"A slow learner, obviously. I repeat the question."

He slapped the side of Painter's head, patronizingly, like an adult cuffing a recalcitrant child.

Painter wheezed, decades of dietary and alcohol abuse rattling in his frame. "Fuck you, bastard. I've slept with a gun under my pillow for the last twenny years, you know what I'm sayin'? You think a fucking schoolboy in fancy dress scares *me*?"

He lurched at Wilde again.

Danny gazed at the empty streets outside, yellow lights passing by overhead, blown litter and stacks of empty packaging; a bleak panorama.

He sighed and said, under his breath, "This is such a waste of time. What am I doing here?" He grabbed the car radio. "Dispatch? Detective Sergeant Danny Everard. Listen, it's quiet as the grave out here. There's a warehouse complex up ahead I'm gonna check out, but I'm not too hopeful. I think you can pull the black-and-whites for now."

He hung up the radio, lit a cigarette, and drove on.

Painter had taken a heavy beating. He was bloodied and bruised, his right eye cut and closing up, a thin, viscous strand of blood swaying from his mouth. He staggered from side to side, gravity and disorientation pulling his body in all sorts of directions. He cut an almost comical figure. But he still refused to say what Wilde wanted to hear, and Wilde's temper was rising.

He punched Painter in the gut, solid but yielding enough, and said, "Now what have you got to say, you son of a bitch?"

Painter gasped, "Nah, man, *you* the son of a bitch. Your mama, I had her working for me only last night."

Wilde kicked him in the ribcage. "What have you got to say?"

"Yeah, she was *gooood*. Those truckers, man, those greasy fat fucks, they couldn't get enough of that old bitch."

Wilde spun and kicked Painter, bang, right under the chin. His head snapped back and his eyes rolled to whiteness. Waters and Whitman gasped. Painter reeled backward and fell heavily to the ground.

Wilde stood over him, saying, "This is only going to get worse, you piece of shit. Answer my question."

Painter peered up at him, struggling to see through injured eyes. He dredged a residual flare of defiance out of somewhere and flipped his tormentor the bird, saying, "There's your...answer...whoreson..."

Wilde's eyes flashed white and furious, his head tilted back; he produced a low moan, somewhere at the back of his throat, and stomped in, over the prone body, bringing down a frenzied barrage of kicks to Painter's head and torso. He looked out of control; Waters turned to Whitman, fear behind his mask, and shook his head.

Wilde stamped, slammed his weight down like a hammer and panted, "What...have you...got to...say...now! Say it! Now! *Answer* me!"

The others acted finally, rushing forward. Whitman caught his friend under the arms and hoisted him back, as Wilde's legs kicked frantically in mid-air. Waters stood before the pimp, tried to make himself look big by spreading his arms, and shouted, "*Don't*! Stop it. You'll kill him."

Wilde heaved, sucking in oxygen, but didn't struggle against his constraints. His body slackened and his eyes closed, sleepy lids scrolling over the tiredness. He muttered, "Mother...mother-fucking...son of a..."

Whitman relaxed his grip a little and spoke in a soft, consolatory voice. "Yeah, he's learned his lesson, man. He's done. Look at him, man, he's..."

Gone. The three of them turned, realization dawning slow and simultaneous, to catch a fleeting glimpse of Painter's kicking heels as he exited the room. Wilde pointed to the equipment.

"Gather up that stuff and get out. Go the back way. I'll meet you by the van. Move!"

Waters said, "What about...?"

"He can't travel too fast. I'll get him. Now go."

Wilde ran toward the door, stopping as he reached it and calling over his shoulder, "Hey! My shoes! Don't forget my fucking shoes!"

Wilde moved. He chased Painter down dark corridors, legs pumping like pistons, every sinew strained in a bid to make up the deficit. He could see the man ahead, turning each corner before him, a shadow scurrying continually out of sight, but he could tell he was gaining—Painter was hurt badly. Wilde tried to breathe through his nose, tried to conserve energy, but it was hard, dual demands weighing down, physiological and psychological. The machine, the corpus, would tire eventually, would have to, letting him down as it wound down; the mind, meanwhile, struggled to control an escalating anxiety, to maintain an effective equilibrium.

Keep breathing, you asshole. Deep and steady.

Wilde moved faster. Then he moved too fast and slipped, his bare feet cold and smooth on the floor. He regained his balance, turned a corner and saw, down a long corridor, Painter standing at a window. The pimp saw him too, scared now, dread on his toughened face. He caught his breath and grabbed the window frame and yelled and jumped...

Danny, about to give up on a lost cause, irritated with himself and with the hangover beginning to settle in his system, rolled slowly around a corner, one second before a heavyset man in a vest erupted from within the building in a hail of glass. He rolled, bleeding and semi-conscious, away from the warehouse wall. Danny didn't react for a moment, didn't even stop the car; he slowed fractionally, without knowing about it, as his sluggish brain played catch-up with the sensory evidence.

Jesus Christ. That's the guy.

He braked hard, at last, leaping from his car to approach the injured man, the car door swinging loose in the glum light. He crouched over Painter's insensible body, gingerly rolling him onto his back. The man was a mess—severe bruising on most of his face; nasty-looking cuts on face and shoulders, presumably from the glass; one eye pounded shut and his mouth a morass of saliva and dark, glutinous blood. Danny looked up, into space, just thinking, working out his best options, and Wilde appeared at the window. Danny almost did a double take, like a clumsy actor in an obvious sitcom. Wilde froze for an instant, nowhere to hide. Their eyes met.

Jesus Christ. That's him. That's *the* guy.

Then Wilde was gone. Danny was still stunned—reveling in this fantastic stroke of luck, afraid to believe in it—but finally snapped out of it, rushing to the car and grabbing the radio.

"This is Detective Sergeant Danny Everard, 14th Precinct. I need back-up immediately. I repeat, immediately. I'm at a

warehouse complex in Red Hook, somewhere near the water...
Near Beard Street? Fuck...trace it with the car GPS. I'm in
pursuit; suspect has run inside the building. Probably armed and
definitely dangerous. Send back-up and an ambulance. There's
an injured man lying outside the building—he looks okay, but it's
hard to tell. Alright, I'm gone."

Danny moved. He sprinted to the window and pulled himself
through it, cutting three fingers on the shards of glass, flinching,
pain searing but mercifully brief, ignoring the pain and running,
hard.

About 30 yards ahead Wilde was sprinting and yelling into the
microphone clipped to his collar: "Guys, get the fuck out. There's
a cop—he's seen me—he's right behind me. Get to the van and
get out. I'll meet you—usual place—move, move!"

He turned a corner into a corridor, the long dismal expanse of
empty space stretching before him. It was difficult to see in this
light; the fear of cracking his shin or slicing open his bare foot on
discarded metal loomed large. Wilde kept running. A few
seconds later, Danny skidded around the corner in pursuit, legs
splayed underneath him like a novice ice-skater. He righted
himself and *moved*: chasing Wilde up flights of stairs, down
echoing iron walkways, through eerie, empty rooms.

His prey was tiring, Danny could tell, though he himself felt
energized, infused with the adrenaline intoxication of pursuit—
of danger. He was gaining ground. Wilde glanced back
occasionally, his face a black smudge with barely discernible
pinpoints of eyeball. Danny raised his gun sporadically, but
couldn't find a clean shot; besides, he was reluctant to shoot
someone in the back. He took his supporting left hand off the
gun and ran, swinging the weapon in his right hand like a limb
extension.

Then Wilde was gone, again. Danny stopped, confused, his
heart pumping, every nerve set on edge. He blinked, squinted

into the blackness. Okay, Everard. Keep it cool. Keep it together. He turned another, indistinguishable corner, coming to the foot of a stairwell, and Wilde crashed down on him from a hiding-space above, yelling wildly, a wordless challenge. They both landed heavily on the floor and Danny's gun clattered away, out of sight. He tried to punch but the other man had pinned his arms to the wet concrete. Danny hoisted upward with his hips, grunting with the effort, and Wilde rolled away.

Danny sprang to a standing position, readied, hyper-aware, and Wilde kicked him behind the right knee. His leg buckled but didn't collapse, and Danny thought, How did he do that so fast? Then Wilde was on him again, two fast punches to the ribs, left-right. Danny wheezed, tried to blank his discomfort, swung with eyes closed, and landed a lucky blow. Wilde took a step back, a little disoriented, and Danny moved in, punching him hard on the temple. Now Wilde was more than a little disoriented; he raised a hand to his head and groaned, almost inaudibly. Danny leaned in, grasping for the balaclava. His hand scrabbled on wool, damp with sweat, his index and middle fingers straining for the eyeholes. Pull off his face; take away the fucker's protection.

Wilde pulled his head back and smacked Danny on the nose with his palm, pushing him away. Pain, sharp and lucid, ran up the center of Danny's face. He squeezed his eyes shut, wiped tears with the back of his hand. He shook his head and vision returned. Wilde was 15 feet away now, bending over, lifting something. Danny sprinted forward, slowed, spotted a lead pipe gathering dust next to a small heap of rubbish and rubble. He stooped, grabbed, and swung the pipe upward, meeting Wilde's counter-strike with a thin steel pole. Metal on metal, clanging loudly and reverberating through their hands. Danny dropped his weapon, his hands trembling, promptings of nausea in his head. Wilde grabbed him by the jacket lapels, throwing him into the dark. Danny slid along the ground and then he saw it—his gun, three feet away, almost invisible. Lucky, Danny boy, lucky.

He crawled, reached for it, turned, and aimed. He shouted, breathing heavily, "*Stop*! Just...right there. Don't move, man, please. I *will* shoot you."

Wilde held his breath—then released again when Waters appeared from nowhere and placed a gun to Danny's temple. He said softly, "Kick it over to him. Slowly. I don't want to hurt you, but he's leaving here with me."

Danny hesitated, bone-tired and half-crazy, and did as he was commanded. Wilde lifted the gun. He smiled at Danny, took a few steps forward, bent down, clutched Danny's head, and kissed him hard on the forehead. Danny thought he heard himself say "What?" in astonishment before Waters cracked him on the skull, sending him to the ground and unconsciousness.

As his vision faded and his mind tuned out, he heard Wilde speak: "I'm pissed 'cause I told you to get the hell out...but I'm glad you didn't listen."

Danny stretched out a hand, but they were beyond his reach. He slumped into oblivion.

2010

'Mm. That was nice.'

'It was. It was really nice. ...God, I hate talking about it straight after doing it.'

'Aw, sorry, babes. I'll shut up.'

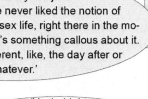

'No, no, it's not you, Courtney. It's just...I dunno, I don't... I've never liked the notion of people discussing their sex life, right there in the moment. You know? There's something callous about it. Mechanical. It's different, like, the day after or whatever.'

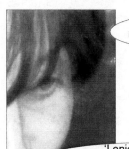

'Yeah. Light me a cigarette, would you?'

'Sure. ... Bleurgh. That *taste*. I don't know how you enjoy those things. I'm not even gonna start on how they'll kill you.'

'I enjoy lots of things that are bad for me. Ha ha, like you. You can keep doing that if you like.'

'Oh, yeah? This? You like this?'

'Mmmm.'

'Hey, hey, careful with the cigarette. These sheets cost me at least ten bucks.'

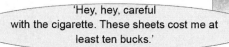

'I'll be careful.
...How're your parents?'

'They're
great, yeah. Gone to – where
is it? – Sicily on holidays at the moment.
...I'd like to travel again.'

'Uh-huh?
Didn't you go all over Europe with
Robert that time?'

'Yeah, I know.
But I wanna go to more places. It's
a big world, darling.'

'It *is* a big world.
It's a big, crazy, messed-up world.'

'Hey,
how profound of
you, Courtney. *Ow.* That
hurt.'

'You
deserved it. And
you've stopped doing
what you were doing.'

'Sorry, sorry.
Forgive me, please. ...Yeah, I reckon I'm
gonna travel some more.'

'Mm?'

'I read
about... This guy went to Thai-
land, right? To one of those resort towns? Horrible, really seedy place. And the guy was just... He was
shocked, he was horrified. He felt so bad for the people
there, the women involved in...you know. The whole
sex industry over there.'

'Yeah?
So why did he go?'

'Because he
wanted to live out his convictions.
That's pretty much... To give force to how he felt. That's
what he told the Thai police. Isn't that so cool? *Man.* I
totally respect that.'

'Sure. Good for him. Most of us would never bother. So what happened?'

'He got arrested. For beating up on some asshole tourist shacked up in a hotel room with a few local girls.'

'What, kids? Urgh, this is a horrible story.'

'Nah, they weren't kids. I say girls, I mean they were, like, young women. The guy, the tourist, he wasn't a pedophile or anything. Just your common-or-garden asshole.'

'So why…? I'm sorry. What happened?'

'He just picked this guy at random and beat the shit out of him. On a point of principle. For his attitude to the local women. For coming over there and choosing them like fruit at a market. He didn't like the guy's attitude.'

'Right. Well, I can't say I disagree with the principle, but… Jesus. He as-saulted him? That's…kinda harsh.'

'No, Courtney, you're right. Totally. But it's an inter-esting story, isn't it? That… To have that force of will. That, sort of, *trust* in your ideals. Like you'd do anything for the right reason.'

'So go on. What happened to him? The force of will guy.'

'He got ar-rested, eventually deported. Dunno what happened after that.'

'And what, is that your plan, baby? Go to Thailand and beat up on some kerb-crawlers? Is that it? Huh? Mr. Tough Guy?'

'Hey, hey. Stop tickling. You know I hate to be tickled. And will you please watch it with that cigarette?'

Chapter 8

Media circus

"OKAY. Let me go through this again; hard to get things right, you know, with my head like this. The warehouse is owned by a legitimate holding company who've let it lie dormant for…how many years?"

Danny nursed a cup of hot tea and nursed his head at the same time, sitting at a scarred table in the station briefing room. He'd often thought of it as a sort of operations room but that wasn't quite accurate, either. Sure, this was a focus point, a sort of central nervous system for cop intelligence, but all the bulletin boards and whiteboards and files and bustle in the world couldn't mask one salient fact—this building was not where most of the operating took place. "Operation": an action, process, activity, effort, undertaking. It all took place out there, Danny believed, on the streets and in people's houses and wherever else the trail led you. And, of course, it also took place *in* there: in his head, where his mind was busy working, even now, as the lingering effects of painkillers exerted a torpid drag.

Three of his fingers had been stitched and bandaged, and they still hurt. He was bruised and pissed, and pissed at the bruises. Captain Harte stood at a small window with a grubby frame and said, in a tone of deep resignation, "Many years, Danny. Many, many years."

"So these guys just walked in there and used it, huh?"

Harte turned to him. "Sure. Do you know how many disused warehouses there are in New York? How quickly you can break into one? How infrequently anyone bothers to check on them? How easily you can find out the owner's name, the building's history…"

Danny waved his hand impatiently. "Okay, okay. Point taken. And the voices on those videotapes: you say they're untraceable?"

"Completely and utterly. They're ghosts, my young friend."

"But of course they are. Any luck tracing the van?"

"Uh-uh. Stolen last night, found torched near the Brooklyn

Bridge this morning. Ghosts, I told you."

Danny said wearily, "Fingerprints? Fibers? Nothing?" He paused; a mental click. "The pimp. Can he identify any of them?"

"No, no, and no again. Our sleazy friend is currently lying comatose in a hospital bed, and if these fellows are as careful and well organized as they seem, then no, he won't be able to tell one from the other, even if he does wake up. What about you? Anything recognizable about their voices, accents? You got pretty up-close to one, right?"

"Nah. They're using...I don't know what. Some sort of contraption—worn around the neck, I'd guess—it lowers the voice octave, distorts it somehow. He doesn't sound the way he sounded last night, if you follow me."

Harte shifted his considerable bulk to a position directly in Danny's sight line, and said, "We do have one thing. I don't know how much help this is gonna be, or even if it makes any sense to you." He closed his eyes, formulating the words, remembering them. "'She lies and says she still loves him, can't find a better man.'" Harte looked at Danny. "Well?"

Danny frowned. "Well what?"

"Does that mean anything to you?"

"James, I'm..." Danny laughed. "I don't know. What are you talking about? What is that?"

"We found it. In the warehouse, written on Coronado's shirt—that's the pimp's name. Scrawled across it in red lipstick. And we're damn sure *he* didn't write it."

Danny nodded and said, "Ah. Right. Another message, then." He sighed. "I don't... I haven't a fucking clue what that is, or where it's from. I'll run it on the internet later. Might...turn up something, or..." He reached for a pen and scribbled the lines into a notebook, then tore out the page and fixed it into his shirt pocket. "'She lies and says she loves him, can't find a better man.' That it?"

"'Says she *still* loves him.' The rest is right." Harte steepled his elegant fingers and placed them to his lips, saying, "Alright. So how do things stand? At first we had one isolated incident; now a pattern has obviously been established. These definitely aren't college students we're dealing with, am I right?"

Danny nodded in agreement.

"Okay. I'm gonna give you two officers to help with the legwork," Harte continued. "Norris and Singh; they're good kids. They can run checks for you, source information, all that. If things don't start to come into focus within a week or so, we'll expand the operation further."

"Uh-huh."

"Thing is, we're undermanned at the moment—you know this yourself—and too many other things need looking into. It's a terrible thing to say but nobody has died here yet, so I can't justify pulling someone off another case. I can't spare you the men right now, but I'll make it happen if we need to. Alright?"

"Sure."

"So keep on it. But report directly to me, Danny." Harte tapped his chest a few times for emphasis. "I need full control over this thing. It's… I've seen this sort of thing before. It's like something out of a goddamn movie. The press loves it, they sell it like it's the latest blockbuster, and the public just goes off the edge. What do you think?"

Danny took a sip of tea and said, "That's fine. Could I just suggest, one: interviews with anyone involved in video or film production—they seem to have access to professional equipment."

Harte nodded.

"And two," Danny said, "a round-up of anyone—male or female, but leaning more toward male—with a history of radical views on gender, misogyny, homophobia, sexual exploitation, that sort of thing. That's the one defining feature here, James: they're not just picking their targets out of thin air. They're random, but within strictly defined parameters."

"Go on."

"Well, think about it: they've chosen a bunch of yuppie assholes playing rough with two call-girls, a so-called 'fag-basher', and a vicious pimp. I mean, you *know* about this guy Coronado, this pimp; Christ, you were probably secretly grateful to them for kicking his ass."

Harte wagged his finger. "Uh-uh. Don't even go *near* that one, Danny."

"Alright, alright. The point is: well, the point is the point. The point they're making. They're selectively punishing members of society—men—who they believe are abusive, intolerant, anti-gay, anti-women, and so on and so on. They're like...they're like Germaine Greer crossed with Charles fucking Bronson."

They both laughed. Harte moved to a filing cabinet five feet away and began gathering the papers scattered on top of it. He said, "There's a disturbing image. Alright, Danny: get on it. Anyone with a history for this type of thinking—online, magazines, college newspapers, activist groups, whatever. But for Christ's sake, be subtle about it. I don't want some poor bastard hauled over the coals just because he wears sandals and has read *The Female Eunuch*, okay?"

Danny mimed the act of note-taking, exaggerated concentration on his face, and said, "Arrest all sandal-wearers carrying copies of *Female Eunuch*. Gotcha. Should I be extra careful if they've got full beards?"

"Always with the kidding around."

"Sorry, James. I'm just..." He leaned his chair back, let his head drop down, ran a hand over his eyes. "I'm fucking drawing a blank here, you know? I don't...*know* enough."

"Well, what do you know?"

Danny breathed out slowly and returned to a proper sitting position. "I know...that they're dangerous, that they're young—well, I think they're young. I don't know what they want, exactly, but I know they're ruthless and driven in getting it. And I know—no; I *feel*—that they're not killers."

"Oh, yeah? Mr. Coronado might disagree with you if he doesn't wake up soon, but...why do you say that?"

"They had me, James. The smaller one—he had me, bang, gun at my temple, good night sweet prince. But all he wanted was the release of his friend. He had me and he let me go." Danny stood and stretched his back, making slow, lazy movements, swiveling around. "I suppose I'm grateful for that, but I can tell you one thing: I won't make the same mistake."

He sat in the briefing room for ten minutes after Harte left, mulling things over, touching his bruises, gathering his strength. And maybe reveling in it a little, he admitted: reveling in the dissatisfaction, the frustration, the nagging sense that events were still taking place somewhere he was not, and he was still just reacting to them, arriving at the heart of things a fraction too late. But misery was okay, Danny thought; unhappiness and irritation and anger, these weren't the worst things in the world. Negative feelings could drive you on, keep you going.

He stood and darted to the door, and Patrick Broder was there when he opened it. Danny started, thinking for a moment that he was hallucinating, the analgesics continuing to mess up his mind. But Patrick had started, too, out of surprise and perhaps a little uncertainty, and Danny knew he wasn't dreaming.

He smiled and said, "Jesus. Patrick. What are you...?" He stopped and beckoned his visitor inside. "Sorry, that's... Where are my manners? 'What are you doing here?' Hell! What a way to welcome a guest!"

Patrick laughed and stepped in, gazing about the room with a detached sort of interest, and placed a package on a desk. "No, no. It's totally my fault. I should have phoned or... I know it seems a little weird, me calling round to you." He laughed self-consciously. "The front desk told me I'd find you here. Guess I sort of bullshitted my way in. Told 'em I had an important package for you from Network 4."

Danny smiled. "And do you?"

"Kind of. It's from Cath and me. Oh, and apologies, by the way, that she couldn't come herself. We heard about what happened last night—that you'd been hurt. She *insisted* we buy you something to cheer you up. You know what women are like. That sweet nurturing instinct." He gestured at the package on the desk, medium-sized and oblong and wrapped in pearl-white paper. "So—dah-daah. Here, open it."

Danny took the package and tore a hole in the paper. He snorted in laughter and said, "Did you know what was in this?"

"Yeah," Patrick drawled slyly. "Yeah, I suggested it. Thought it might inspire you."

Danny flipped the parcel around so Patrick could see the inside: a box set of the *Dirty Harry* movies, from the original to *The Dead Pool*. They both smiled.

"Right," Danny said. "A vigilante cop who'll stop at nothing. Just the sort of role model the department encourages."

"Hey, know your enemy, right? You must become what you fight, and all that."

Danny placed the package back on the desk. "Yeah, thanks for that, *sensei*. Nah, it's cool, it's great. Thanks, to both of you guys."

"No problem." Patrick half-sat on one of the desks, scanning the room absentmindedly. "So you wouldn't approve of all that stuff, then? That Dirty Harry approach?"

Danny fumbled in his jacket pocket for a pack of chewing gum. "Are you kidding? Off the record, of *course* I approve. What cop wouldn't want to just go out there and fuck up the first rapist or child-killer who crossed his path? Just fuck him right up. Not all the time. You don't feel like that all the time. But we're human beings, Patrick. It's a natural instinct."

"The instinct for revenge."

"Yeah, but I don't know if it's all about revenge. I mean, it is to an extent, but it's about justice, too. Bringing about a proper resolution." He squashed a piece of gum into his mouth and spoke around it. "I don't know if you… Am I explaining myself properly here? Okay, it's like this: to do something like that, something frenzied and brutal, you know, sometimes that can feel warranted. It can feel *right*."

Patrick looked skeptical. "Hmm. I dunno. Sounds like you're trying to justify to yourself. Like you *do* have the thirst for vengeance, but you're dressing it up as justice. Like you're not being honest with…"

Danny shook his head and said, "Nuh-uh. Because the thing is this: I'd never do it. I might think it, and even agree with it sometimes, but I wouldn't *do* it. Because those other times, when you don't feel like that? Those times you realize that vengeance is wrong. It's wrong, and unjust, and ultimately it hurts you more than them, anyway."

"Right, you're gonna quote that old Chinese proverb now: 'The man who sets out for revenge should start by digging two graves.'"

Danny laughed. "I might. Shit. Chinese proverbs in one ear and your Zen master wisdom in the other… I mean, it's complicated, I admit, but I think, fundamentally… The law is all we have, you know? The rule of law. This contract between every member of our society. And I *know* it doesn't always work. Trust me, I know. But for good or bad, we have to hold onto that. Everything else is just…"

"Happy chaos?"

"Chaos, yes. Happy, I'm not so sure."

Danny began pulling on his jacket. He said, "Listen, I'm sorry. I *am* being rude, but I just have a world of stuff to get working on. Is that okay?"

Patrick hopped off his perch and said, "God, yes, of course. *I'm* sorry, I shouldn't be holding you up like this."

They moved to the door. Danny said, "Thanks for the gift. It's much appreciated. And tell Cathy I said thanks, would you?"

"Sure. And thank *you* for that, uh, little discussion. It was...enlightening."

"Aw, don't get all Zen on me again. Please. It's too early in the day for profundity."

Patrick laughed. Danny reached for the doorknob and turned it, then held the door ajar. He said, "Hey, by the way. Maybe you can... Hold on." He reached for the piece of paper with the lines Harte had quoted. "'She lies and says she loves him, can't find a better man.' Don't suppose you happen to know where those lines are from?"

Patrick nodded, an amused frown creasing his forehead. "Sure. It's Pearl Jam. You know, the grunge band? Or were they a little after your time?"

Danny smiled and said, "Oh, yeah. It all ended for me when Elvis died. Yes, I know Pearl Jam. Which song is this one?"

"It's just called *Betterman*. And that's the chorus: 'She lies and says she still loves him, can't find a better man. She dreams in color, she dreams in red, can't find a better man...' And so on. Great song. Why do you ask, anyway?"

Danny shook his head, a loose, tired movement. He folded the paper back into his shirt and said, "Ah...doesn't matter. Forget about it. Just another piece of an impossible fucking puzzle."

He laughed to himself. Patrick smiled and said, "Hey, don't say that. Nothing is impossible. With enough will and dedication? *Nothing* is impossible."

Danny smiled as well. "I hope you're right, Patrick. I sincerely do."

A media circus: a phenomenon wherein the press and radio and television follow a rising news story en masse, like the retinue of attendants in the train of a king of old. They follow it, then pass it out, forcing it into unexpected shapes and directions, forward or back but always, constantly moving. It's a symbiotic relationship, a self-fulfilling prophecy, where the story itself becomes the story, the progress of its narrative assuming a superior importance to the reality being played out on screens and front pages. It's a circus, and everyone wants a front row seat.

And Danny was right at the center of this one. Now he stood, bruised and disheveled, addressing the ranked masses of the media outside the station house doors. He said, "Look, look, all I'm gonna say at this point is, yes, these three incidents are, we believe, connected; and no, we're not 'stumbling in the dark', as my esteemed friend from News 24 suggests. We have a number of leads, and feel we're very close to a resolution of this case. Thank you..."

Cut to a daily current affairs show: two analysts propounding theories about the gang, talking across each other. A fleshy woman with hard-set hair said, "Well, obviously, there is some sort of political angle to this that we just haven't seen yet. People do not just go out and, and, beat up people for no apparent reason..."

A swarthy man in a beautiful suit leaned across and said patronizingly, "With all due respect, Cecilia, you can't have been paying too much attention to the news recently, because there *is* a reason for these attacks. I mean, they've *told* us the reason— they've spelled it out on videotape! Ha ha ha..."

Cut to edited footage of the first two attacks, playing across all channels, usually after the evening watershed—Hudson and Steve hanging outside the window with their groins digitally blurred; Wilde interrogating Tommy; the words, pulsing and insistent: "Karma TV—it could be you."

And Bailey and Cathy, watching it all unfold in the screening room, gaping, helpless. He sat on the low leather couch; she paced the room restlessly, stressed out, chewing on a nail. She said, "Shit. How the...? *Shit*. How did those fuckers get that footage so fucking fast?"

"Goddamn unscrupulous bastards. I'll tell you what this has got, Cathy: this has got the reek of conspiracy about it. Yeah, conspiracy. It's a set-up to, to, to discredit us, to blacken our..."

Cathy glared at him. "Oh, shut *up*, Jonathon."

Cut to a new entry appearing at the top of "The Asphalt World (Musings, Meditations and Mourning of Modern Culture)", an online blog written by a 19-year-old media theory student with an IQ of 184 who looked like a younger, even skinnier Jeff Goldblum.

"Holy freakin' schemoley, Asphalt World citizens. This just popped into my inbox not one hour ago. Not even sure if I'm legally allowed use it. Oh, to hell with it... I've uploaded it to the main page; click on the link for 'Coronado.mpg.' This *claims* to be real footage of the 3W vigilantes beating some manners into their latest pupil—a nasty dude with a real sweet attitude.

"I stress: claims. But you know the amount of bullshit on the 'net. Personally I'm not sure: there are no credits or smart-ass commentary like on the previous two—it's just video footage, barely edited at all. But then again, how do we know the previous two were real anyway? And not just alternate versions doctored and released by the NYPD? We don't, we can't, we know, we don't know.

"What are you asking me for? *I* don't know. Go watch it and judge for yourselves."

Cut to a vox pop on a chilly street, a wobbly handheld camera, the furry outdoor microphone sneaking into shot sporadically.

A nervous-looking thirtysomething woman wrung her hands and said, "They're criminals. And what are the police doing about it? They're criminals and thugs. Probably part of some sort of street gang..."

A kid with thick hair over his eyes giggled dumbly, then

composed a serious face and drawled, "Uh...I dunno. Like, I think it's kinda cool, that they're doing what they wanna do... But on the other hand, it's probably, like, illegal? So...I gotta say, I'm conflicted, man..."

A florid-faced old gent, waves of silver hair and year-round tan, blustered at the camera, "My God, what is the world coming to? When respectable young men can't feel safe in their own homes. In their own homes! Without these psychopathic terrorists invading their privacy and doing these unspeakable things. Yes, *terrorists*! It's a world gone mad..."

Then back to the male studio presenter, grinning inanely: "As you can see, there seems to be some divergence of opinions among the public on this iss..."

Benjamin van Horne sat with his wife on the couch, cuddling, their faces bright in the soft light of the TV screen. He bit down on his lower lip and smiled at her with a profound love in his eyes; she smiled back.

Cut to a studio debate bearing all the hallmarks of low-rating, defiantly intellectual programming: minimalist sets, sparse lighting, earnest men and women arguing their point with extravagant hand movements.

A young man with a pleasant, sincere face said, "Well, while their methods are somewhat dubious, I can't say I necessarily disagree with their aims, though I know that's probably not the politic thing to say..."

An intense young woman in a knitted skullcap and black dinner jacket came in: "Finally. *Thank* you. And can I just add to that, you know, one less pimp or gay-basher in the world, that's a good thing, to my mind. Pity there weren't more guys out there like that."

The oily host, feigning outrage, spluttered, "What...!? Are you seriously suggesting, Anna, that vigilantism is acceptable? That you *defend* this sort of behavior? I have to say, I'm shocked..."

"Hey," she replied, "it's like Teddy Roosevelt said: sometimes people just don't listen if you speak nice to them, okay? Sometimes you gotta do some damage with a big stick first..."

Her voice carried from a TV set, fixed to a bracket near the top of the wall, in Tommy's hospital room, as his mother sat, teary-eyed and broken-down, next to her unconscious son.

Cut to the boyish presenter of *CrimeSpot*, a popular show covering major crime stories, local and international: "Again, I must warn you: the following material may be offensive to some people. It contains violence and strong language, and is recommended only for mature viewers. Okay, let's roll the tape."

Coronado's broad, strong face, taking over the screen, like his hatred and anger were expanding to fill it, spittle flying from his mouth as he screamed, "Yeah, I (bleep) killed a few! You happy now, you crazy (bleep)? I beat one to death with my golf club, and I let the other die of a (bleep) overdose!"

Then Wilde hammering the pimp's belly with both fists, grunting, "Now what have you got to say, you son of a (bleep)?" Coronado replying, "Nah, man, *you* the son of a (bleep)... Those truckers, man, those greasy fat (bleep), they couldn't get enough of that old (bleep)."

In close-up, right in there, almost intimate: Wilde spinning and kicking, Coronado's eyes rolling, his head jolting back, crashing to the ground. Silence. The presenter stringing the tension out.

He cleared his throat as the camera returned to him: "Well. Clearly an *extremely* serious incident. Jim, if I could turn to you first..."

Cut to a news anchorman with a smarmy, toothy smile and angular jaw-line. He said, "And on a lighter note, one gay New York nightclub is reported to have begun running what they term '3W' nights in honor of, and I quote, 'this group's gallant defense of a gay man against unprovoked attack by bigoted enemies of society. Janet Kidney is there now…"

They went over to Janet, a mousy woman with auburn hair, standing outside the front doors of Klub Khan, holding a microphone up to the face of a brawny man with a shaved head—presumably the club's owner, though no identifying panels appeared on screen.

The man smiled and said, "Yeah, all I gotta say is, too many people stand by and let this stuff go down all the time in our society. But like their namesakes, these guys showed courage, inventiveness, and belief in what was right. And, Mr. Wilde?" He raised an eyebrow at the camera. "Any time you feel like dropping by, I can *guarantee* you a warm reception."

There were hoots and hollers in the background as Janet was hugged by a big group of men; she shrugged and smiled giddily. Amy and Dorothy watched it from their apartment—Amy on the couch, Dorothy on the ground at her feet. The younger girl glanced up at Amy with a questioning look; Amy gave her a small smile and looked at the screen again.

Cut to an interview with a skinhead in a black t-shirt, his face half-filling the screen. A name-plate underneath read, "Eric Moose—Aryan People's Liberation Front."

He grabbed the proffered microphone and declared, "We at the APLF take heart from the actions of the 3W Gang. For too long our country has been over-run by unhealthy and criminal foreign elements, spreading disease, selling drugs, terrorizing decent, law-abiding citizens in their homes. Now the way has been shown for a better future for our children, the way of purging the streets of all the scum. The hookers and drug-dealers, the beggars and crooks: we're coming for *you*."

Moose pointed at the camera and made an "X" with his fisted arms.

Cut to a professorial-looking man wagging his finger as he made his argument on another discussion show. An on-screen name-plate read, "Jerome LaVey, political activist."

He said, "This is patently—*patently*—yet another smear campaign by the white establishment against black people. By abducting Tommy Richmond and making these allegations about him, they are making a contrived link between homophobia and all young black males..."

The presenter, a timid, unimposing man in an ill-fitting suit, countered, "Well, I do believe that Mr. Richmond's gang came from a number of ethnic backgrounds, Jerome..."

"Yes, and that's exactly it. That's exactly my point. Why, in that case, was it the *black* man who was chosen? Why not the Hispanic or the Chinese or, God forbid, the white man? I see this every day in my work on the ground, at community level, and I can tell you..."

Clifford Hudson sat with some friends around a bar table as Jerome LaVey ranted in the background. Someone had cracked a joke and they all laughed heartily. Hudson remembered where he was and belatedly joined in.

Cut to a cheesy, grinning presenter, hovering above an onscreen graphic: "You the Jury. The 3W Gang: heroes or villains? Vote now!!"

He chuckled, for no apparent reason, and said, "Well, there you can see it, right now, on your TV screens. Our vote of the week: 'The 3W Gang: heroes or villains?' As always, *you* decide, and it's as easy as one, two, three—just call the number at the bottom right-hand corner and follow the recorded instructions..."

Wilde clicked off the TV and sank back into his armchair. The headache was getting worse; he had felt alright earlier that day, but now there was a throbbing pain in his temple, spikes of pain rising and falling in time with his pulse. He rested three fingers lightly against his right temple and clutched his balaclava in the other hand. He kneaded the garment, squashing the wool against itself.

He stared at the black-gray blankness of the dead screen, then blinked the pain from his head, reached for his cell phone, and keyed in a message: "MESSAGE GETTIN CONFUSED. NEED 2 EXPLAIN OURSELVS PROPERLY. LET PEOPLE KNOW. SEND IT FOR 11.45 AM TOMORO." He selected Waters' number from the database and pressed "OK", and his message flew.

"It Does Not Scan" Poetry Quarterly

Vol. XI Summer 2006

Open page: where *you* submit
and *we* publish

"emasculate" by
Fingal O'Flahertie

the greasy black street
a shiny sidewinder glowing home
as the zombies shuffle by
bellies full and aching for another hour
please let us stay another hour
and vampires slit the night
on padded feet
gurgling laughs from another
place
and they dance alone
for the women are crying
their scraping rising cry
and the dance is done
in black cloth and white stripes
and the blur of high-kicks
and the swish of the air
being cut and bled
and he'll creep away to lie like
children
in the lazy little death
dreams of heroes leaking

like piss into a clammy drain
the staunchest bandage
won't soak the flow
from creaking bones and
hollow heads
and surgeons should prepare
with knives and pins
and cotton buds
and nerves of steel
wipe the cool table clear
and make the cut
filling tanks with thousands
while beautiful women
laugh and drink wine
a toast to the age just passed
may it choke on the sand
and a hope for the gentle fight
in the soothing nights ahead

Chapter 9

We wish to do an interview

CATHY looked tired. Stealing sideways glances at her as they sat on a pretty *chaise longue* in one of Network 4's hospitality rooms, Patrick thought she looked tired. Tiny red veins showed at the side of her eyeball, dark little threads against the blue-white of her eyes. She was under a lot of pressure, he knew that. But, like before, he didn't quite know how to assuage it.

He tried to think of something encouraging to say and then Cathy nullified the need by speaking herself. She breathed heavily and said, "Two days. Two days, and not a whisper."

"No more videotapes?"

She shook her head. "Nothing. Two days and nothing. It's like they're hiding or something. Biding their time."

"Well, maybe that, ah, altercation with Danny spooked them a little," Patrick replied. "You know, like they're scared of being identified now."

"Maybe. I guess so. I don't know." Cathy paused; she twisted her fingers into themselves, stared at her upturned shoes. "Anyway, can we forget about the goddamn 3W Gang for five minutes? How have you been lately?"

She turned and beamed a lovely smile on him, and Patrick thought, Man—the strength of a woman. Never ceases to amaze. Then he remembered that she had asked him a question and said, "Me? Uh...fine. Yeah, I've been okay. I feel sorta bad for you, though."

"Why would you have cause to feel bad for me?"

He shrugged. "Ah, it's just... Y'know, with all this trouble with management. Them blaming you for the tapes being leaked. All that."

Cathy smiled again and patted his leg—a kind, almost maternal gesture, though she wasn't that much older than he. "You're sweet, Patrick. Don't worry. It's not your fault. It'll all blow over soon enough anyway, and we can move smoothly on to the next crisis here at the Network 4 funhouse."

Patrick nodded and gave her hand a brief squeeze. He wanted

to reassure her, to help out, to somehow remove Cathy from this whole situation. But again, there wasn't much he could do right now, except wait for certain things to take their course.

Downstairs, at that moment, a bicycle courier—a thin, pale fellow who bore a striking resemblance to a young Woody Allen—was approaching Jennifer at the reception desk. She looked even more bored than usual, sighing loudly and staring into space, her head rested on one hand. She was considering her options for summer vacation—the beach or a city break in Boston?—when her receptionist sixth sense kicked in and she peripherally noticed the little courier approaching, his bowed, hairy legs showing under fluorescent shorts. Jennifer snapped into an upright position and smiled blandly.

The courier parried with a half-hearted smile of his own and said, "Uh...yeah, hi. I gotta package here for a—just lemme check this—right, a Jonathon Bailey. Could you, like, page him for me?"

Jennifer nodded warily and discreetly pressed a button under her desk. She said, "Uh-huh. No problem. If you could just wait for one moment..."

Less than a minute later two brawny security men rushed into view and effortlessly manhandled the courier to the ground. He kicked with those skinny legs and yelled, "*Hey*! Hey, what the fuck is this? That's not *my* bike parked illegally, if that's what you're thinking..."

One of the security guards spoke into his earpiece: "Yeah, John? We got a courier here. At reception. You better get that cop over here. Yeah, that's the one..."

He looked up and caught Jennifer's eye. He'd always found her very attractive. The security guard posed there, the courier pinioned by his large hands, like a big game hunter proudly displaying his prize. Jennifer perked up and smiled at him. He wouldn't be bad-looking if he grew his hair a little, she thought.

I wonder if he likes the beach?

"Look, I told you already—I don't know nothing about this package. I just ride the fucking bikes, man. I ride the bikes."

Danny rubbed his forehead and the corners of his eyes. He'd known from the moment he stepped into the room that this courier, this Toby Lipnicki, would prove to be an awkward son of a bitch. Danny guessed that the guy had some sort of Napoleon syndrome—the small man's need to prove himself. He was abrasive and confrontational, and he spoke very quickly and very loudly. Danny looked back at him across the desk in a small utility room on Network 4's first floor. The security guard, the one who'd phoned him 20 minutes previously, had ushered him into the room with an urgency that suggested one of two things: either he thought he was on protective detail for the President, or he thought he was the lead in a bang-and-boom movie about a SWAT team. Bonehead, Danny thought; brutal goddamn macho asshole.

"I know that, Mr. Lipnicki," he said. "But what might seem trivial to you might be of massive significance to me, so please, indulge me—run through it again."

Lipnicki looked around and waved a pack of cigarettes in the air. "Okay to smoke in here? I don't wanna get arrested by youse or nothing."

Danny nodded. Lipnicki lit a cigarette and launched into it: "Alright, here it is—*again*—the delivery was paid for, in cash, this morning. I know this 'cause I was on my coffee break at the time, and I seen the guy. I can even tell you the name. Let's see…" He rustled through a sheaf of crumpled papers. "…here it is: N R Graves. That's all I got: N R Graves."

Danny smiled. "Hopefully not prophetic. What did this man look like?"

"He was, uh…pretty ordinary, really. Youngish, pale skin; regular-looking guy. He had on a hooded top, so I don't know about his hair."

"How tall was he?"

"Mmm...not very. Shorter than you. Little bigger than me. Look, I don't know nothing, alright? I was told deliver this package to whatsisname—this guy Bailey—at exactly quarter before noon. And that I did."

Danny nodded and looked at the desk. "Alright. Thanks, Mr. Lipnicki. You're free to go."

Lipnicki rose, gathered his things and said sarcastically, "And gee, thank *you*. Am I gonna get compensated by the Police Department for my loss of time here?"

Danny shot him a withering look; the aggrieved courier slunk away. A young uniformed officer with jet-black hair and a baby face—Norris, one of the two who'd been assigned to Danny—stuck his head in the door. He said tentatively, "Detective? We've checked the package. It's clean, it's fine."

"So what it is?"

Norris stepped into the room. "It's, like, a Dictaphone. You know, for recording voices and stuff?"

"Yep, I know. Bring it on in, Officer Norris."

The officer placed the Dictaphone on the table. Thin; dark-silver rather than black; an old-style mechanical model, not one of the more modern digital ones. Danny took a breath and pressed play—Wilde's voice rang out, tinny but recognizable.

"Good afternoon, Detective Everard. I hope you're feeling better after our brief *contretemps* the other evening. Sorry if I hurt you—you seem a good man, and you're only doing your job. But we couldn't allow you to catch me, or to stop us in what we're doing. You see, we have *our* job to do, too. With that in mind, please instruct Mr. Bailey to call this cell number—nine-one-seven; three-five-nine-seven; four-three-seven—at exactly 12.30pm. We wish to do an interview."

Silence, except for a slight hissing of static. Danny frowned momentarily, a little taken aback, then checked the clock on the wall: it was now 12.10pm. He pocketed the recording device and hauled ass.

The entire place was a frenetic hive of activity: every floor, it appeared, every room, every available space. Danny looked around and thought, Holy shit. And to think how busy the station house sometimes seemed. Floor and technical staff rushed around, racing against time to ready the studio for Bailey's interview with Wilde. Men in earpieces, women holding clapboards, gestures and commands, sound checks and light tests, security huddling among themselves, pointing out certain areas and nodding gravely. Danny let out a long breath and retreated to a quiet corner in the wings. The voice at the other end of his phone was being drowned in the cacophony, the noisy bustle.

He raised his voice a notch and said, "Yeah, a cell phone. I've given your colleague the number. You should be able to triangulate the signal to within a reasonably small area. Gimme something workable here, guys. I'm depending on you. Hold on…" He flipped to a second line. "Yes, Tyler… I said I needed *more* men, godammit, not less. There's been a *what*…? Jesus Christ. Alright. Alright. No, I know it's not your fault. Look, just do what you can. And get back to me as soon as possible."

Danny pointed to Norris and Singh, lurking ten feet away, looking strangely bashful, like schoolboys who've crashed an adult party. Singh was very thin with coffee-colored skin and a persistent expression of deep concentration.

"Okay," Danny said. "Norris, I want you covering this floor and the top level, the management level. Singh, I want you to roam the other floors and the reception area. It would appear that we're a little under-par in terms of manpower, but we'll just have to manage."

Norris coughed into his hand. "Uh, sir?"

"Yes, Officer."

"Sir, I've, ah…that is, Singh and me, we've heard that, uh, that these are pretty dangerous fucking guys, right?" He laughed nervously. "So, uh, so what I'm wondering, sir, is…"

"You're wondering if you're going to be safe. You're wondering if a bomb is going to go off and bring this whole place down. If you should phone your girlfriends now, while you still can."

Norris laughed again, even more embarrassed. Singh remained silent and watchful. Norris said, "Well, uh…yes, sir. That's pretty much it."

Danny leaned toward them and said, "You can calm those fears right away. Okay? This gang hasn't used explosives of any sort, or targeted more than two people at a time, up until now, and I've no reason to suspect that's going to change. I'd be amazed if they even come near this place today—hence their use of a cell phone. You, and Singh and I, are just…insurance. Just in case. Alright?"

Norris nodded, obviously relieved. "Yes, sir. Thank you, sir."

"Now go do your jobs. And stay alert…" Danny smiled mischievously. "…just in case."

In the center of the studio Bailey's make-up was being touched up. He stretched his face into funny shapes as Cathy stood nearby, arguing with the station manager, a barrel-chested egomaniac called Murray Helmore.

She said, "I still think this is a really, really bad idea. It's just giving them what they want, and I have to express my strong disapproval to…"

"Duly noted and remembered, Cathy," Helmore replied. "But you know the rationale behind this: if we go out live, someone listening, someone in their car or walking along the street, might overhear the mysterious Mr. Wilde as he talks. Right? So this whole thing could be ended by lunchtime today. Besides which…"

Bailey said to the make-up girl, his voice slightly distorted by the upward tilt of his jaw, "Do you think you're almost finished there? I really should… Hello! You—guy behind the camera light. Could you redirect it, please? It's right in my goddamn face, I can't see…"

"Come on, Cathy," Helmore continued. "Think of the *ratings*. This is the nearest modern equivalent to getting Oswald for an on-air *tête-à-tête*."

Cathy threw her hands in the air and stalked away, angrily shaking her head. Helmore turned and saw Bailey. He smiled and made the shape of two pistols with his fingers, pointing them at the anchorman.

"*Heeyy*, Jonathon. How you feeling? You ready for this? Your biggest moment in 20 years, baby."

Bailey said dryly, "Sure, Murray. Can't wait." He swallowed what felt like a thick clump of dust in his throat. The light was still in his face, and he couldn't see a damn thing.

The hands on the large, white studio clock moved round slowly: 12.25pm. Patrick and Cathy stood on the sidelines, waiting. She chewed on a fingernail, which seemed so out of character to Patrick that he almost laughed out loud. 12.27pm. Danny stood on the other side, tensed and ready to roll—in what direction, he wasn't sure. He just knew he'd have to be prepared for anything, at the same time convinced that that wasn't possible. He absent-mindedly checked his holster, feeling the reassuring, familiar shape of his gun under his fingers. 12.29pm. Now there was an almost palpable air of expectation, an electric charge of antici-pation crackling through the studio, through the entire building. A communal intake of breath—holding it—unsure glances from person to person—a reassuring nod, a disconcerted shrug.

Then the clock swept past 12.30pm and the red light blinked on. Bailey looked around for a second, like he didn't quite know what to do, then took a deep breath and began talking to camera.

"Good afternoon, and welcome to Network 4 news. It's 12.30,

I'm Jonathon Bailey, and as you're probably aware by now, we're able to bring you, live today, an exclusive interview with the leader of the so-called '3W Gang' which has been making the news headlines over the past week. I've been instructed to call a certain cell phone number to make contact with the gang's leader, codenamed Wilde, so..." Bailey keyed in the number, milking the moment for all its dramatic potential, and paused: a dial tone was heard. "We have a dial tone, and..."

Then a voice was heard, saying, "Mr. Bailey. Very punctual." The reception was slightly fuzzy; a swirling, outer space sort of crackle.

Bailey said, "Uh...thank you. So, uh, Mr. Wilde... Should I call you that, or do you have a first name?"

"Wilde is fine. No 'Mister' required."

"Wilde. Alright. Should I, uh, dictate the course of this conversation, or are there particular questions you want me to ask you?"

"Ask me what the public wants to know; what you want to know. Help explain this to people."

Bailey frowned. He thought for a moment then said, "Alright... Well, I suppose the first question the average viewer would like to ask is: why are you doing this?"

A long pause. "We're doing this...to make a point. That's it in a nutshell. To make a point, and make a statement."

Bailey said flatly, "A statement."

Wilde said, "Simple as that."

The camera operator zoomed in on Bailey's face, slowly, his heavy features enlarging, filling the giant screen which rested high above the counter of an East Village bar. A disparate group of people stood around, holding drinks, uneasy and intrigued. Bailey stared blankly at the watching audience as Wilde's voice rang out over the low background notes of bar chatter.

"We feel...very strongly about certain issues," he began. "But they're what might be termed vague, or 'soft', issues—not, we felt, the sort of thing around which one organizes protest marches or letter-writing campaigns. These are more...subtle, and nebulous; less easily defined. This isn't Ban the Bomb or Free Nelson Mandela; it has a different dynamic."

Bailey said, "Different. Uh-huh. So what, precisely, are these issues?"

"In probable order of immediacy: misogyny, homophobia, general chauvinism. And then the more involved threads which fan out from that: the destructive hypocrisy of this whole 'whore/Madonna' way of thinking, domestic abuse of women, the propagation of violence against gay men, the glass ceiling for professional women, among other things... Have you read *The Beauty Myth*, Mr. Bailey?"

"By Naomi Wolf? No, I'm afraid not."

"Well, in that book she talks about..."

Danny crouched down on the studio floor, speaking softly into his radio. "The sound's fading in and out a little here—I'm guessing they're in a vehicle somewhere... You got that too? Okay, okay, get back to me..."

He crept around the long way, reaching Cathy, touching her arm. She started a little, then smiled in greeting. Danny whispered, "Does it sound funny to you? His voice. Does it sound strange, or...different in any way?"

Cathy shrugged. "I couldn't really say. I mean, it's distorted, isn't it? Some sort of gizmo..."

"Yeah, I know. It just... It's probably nothing. Forget about it."

They both turned toward Bailey again. He had loosened his tie a fraction; a sure sign, to Cathy, that he was genuinely interested in the subject. For a fleeting moment she felt mildly impressed by her boss. Numerous staffers cloistered around the floor, ignoring the no-smoking signs and intently watching Bailey.

He said, "...you're saying is that these things are endemic in our culture?"

Wilde laughed. "Of *course* they are. Jesus. No offense, Mr. Bailey, but you'd have to be a blind imbecile not to see that."

Bailey pouted, embarrassed. Wilde continued, "Look, the whole point is that *we're* the normal ones here, with the normal, rational, well-reasoned *Weltanschauung*. Those others—the gay-bashers and rapists and casual sexists? They're the ones who have problems, whose way of perceiving the world is illogical and vindictive. And terribly screwed-up."

Bailey snorted, "Oh, come on, Wilde, please! You're seriously suggesting that it's...*normal* to go out and send people to the hospital because you disagree with their—how did you phrase it?— '*Weltanschauung*'? To dress up in suits and masks and..."

"Balaclavas and tuxedos, actually. They work far better together. No, it's not normal to do those things simply because nobody has done them before. What we're saying is: maybe it should be."

Bailey sighed, exasperated. "I... Really, I find it hard to..."

A nervous-looking Singh patrolled the upper floors, his hand lightly resting on his gun-butt. The sound of the interview poured out of dozens of TV sets throughout the building, in stereo, in multi-stereo. The cumulative effect of the sound made Singh feel almost nauseous. That, and the sour knot of fear in the base of his gut.

He shook droplets of sweat off the palm of his hand and heard Wilde say, "Look. I'm not gay myself, nor are either of my colleagues. I'm a regular, straight guy. I like sports. I like sex. I drink beer, you know? I look at a pretty girl on the street and, yes, I think of her in a sexual way. In the common parlance, and excuse my language, I think, Wow, I'd like to fuck her. It's natural and biological and harmless."

Bailey winced, a crease of mild panic filling three-quarters of virtually every television screen in the greater New York area.

"What you have to understand here, we're acting on a point of principle. This isn't Hollywood, okay? There was no convenient trigger. You know, nobody close to me has been raped or beaten up or trapped in an abusive marriage, and thank God for that. This isn't about personal revenge. I know that would be easier for you to grasp, if there was some dark event from my past, compelling me to do this. Well, sorry to disappoint. I had a nice childhood, caring parents, different girlfriends, all that. The usual stuff."

Singh gulped, steeled himself. He tried to picture having dinner with his girlfriend that evening, cooking for her, and continued his patrol.

Captain Harte leaned forward, following the interview intently, listening as Bailey said, "You say it's not revenge. And yet you seem so...committed."

Wilde gave a little laugh. "You wanted to say 'zealous' but you were too scared, right...? See, that's my point. You shouldn't *need* personal experience to get angry or passionate, to feel the pull of a moral obligation. It was like a gradual political awakening for us, the very same as for a socialist or Civil Rights activist. The same fundamental sense of justice and fairness, period. That's all there is and that's all you need. You know, I mean, Lenin wasn't impoverished. He was middle-class and he overthrew the whole class system. White people marched for racial equality. You don't have to be a victim of something yourself to empathize."

Harte picked up a pencil and began twirling it absent-mindedly in his fingers.

"And we—as a group and a society—have to draw the line somewhere," Wilde said. "For a man to deny a woman her humanity, simply because she works as a prostitute, is unacceptable. For a group of men to kick another to death because of his sexuality is unacceptable. Every time we hear words like 'slut' and 'tramp' and 'fag' is one time too many. And these are only the obvious manifestations. The subtleties, those cloaked methods of control, they're almost worse. Because nobody seems to recognize that they're there. Or if they do, they just don't care. This is the greatest human rights crime in history, and no one gives a shit."

Danny's body tensed as a communication came through on his earpiece. He said, "Yeah, go ahead. Right... How difficult...? A prepaid phone; right, I expected that. Okay, look, just keep on it. Another few minutes."

Wilde said, "...have been brainwashed into considering themselves lesser beings. Maybe not even consciously, but it's there. It's there every time one woman calls another woman a slut or a whore. Which to me, you know, that's like blacks calling each other 'coon', or Vietnamese talking about 'gooks.' It's just... It makes no sense. It's there every time a woman reads about a rape trial and says, 'Oh, maybe she asked for it.'" He laughed, humorless and bitter. "Jesus Christ! What other serious crime puts the victim on trial as much as the aggressor?" Another long pause. "It's like, in some ways women are their own worst enemies. But ultimately, they're not. It's us. It's men. We're the ones who are doing this, who've brainwashed them. And we're the ones who have to stop it."

Danny tuned out Wilde's voice as another message was relayed. He listened and said, "Yes, I'm still inside... Good. Good. Within four blocks. Excellent. Stay with him, I want his location narrowed down to the nearest ten fucking yards if possible."

He began walking back across the studio, quietly, feet light on the tiled floor.

Wilde's voice carried across the space on wall-mounted speakers: "...opposed to an unjust war, you damage jump jets with hammers or march on Congress. But how do you protest an attitude? What's the recognized symbol for anti-homophobia?

It's…vague and complex, a misfiring neuron hardwired into the consciousness. The normal rules of engagement do not apply."

Bailey gave a non-committal grunt in reply; it almost seemed like he was unwilling to break the flow, the smooth outpouring of angry philosophy.

"And this situation, here it's even more ambiguous than, say, racism or anti-Semitism," Wilde went on. "Racism is recognized by most right-thinking people as unjust, simply *wrong*. Yet the same doesn't apply to misogyny or homophobia. Why? The same people who would abhor the Nazis or apartheid, on the other hand it's all 'fags' and 'bitches', it's all hatred and contempt." A thoughtful pause. "I don't know. Maybe people should think of women and homosexuals as a different race! Right? Maybe then they might stop and think, 'It's not right to treat them like this…'"

Danny reached Norris and tapped his shoulder, making him jump.

"Sorry, kid," Danny said. "Listen: this guy is close, and coming closer. I'm going outside—I won't attract as much attention as you fellas in uniform. Stay in contact. And Norris: you're doing great. Keep it up."

He checked his gun and earpiece. He exited the studio as Wilde continued, "…ideal solution would be to re-engineer the way people think. Not just scare people into behaving, but actually change our society. Our thoughts, and the language we use. Because you know, Mr. Bailey, the effect of language. Deep down, in the back brain, it shapes our attitudes and behavior. But let's face it: we're about 3000 years of evolution away from that point. People aren't gonna change overnight. We know that. We're not naïve."

Now Danny got the surround sound effect as he strode briskly downstairs, Wilde's manifesto bouncing and rebounding around the ether, the volume rising or falling as he passed different speakers. Danny grit his teeth and checked his weapon yet another time.

Wilde declared, "Enough dialogue. Here it is: we believe society needs balance—a sort of enforced karma. Individuals must be punished for their mistreatment of others. Individuals picked at random. And please, don't bother to tell me that it won't stop this behavior. Because I already know, and that doesn't matter. What matters is this balance. An even flow— psychically, socially, culturally, and emotionally." He paused. "It's science. You know the physics theory: for every action, there must be a reaction. Well, we didn't start this; we're just reacting. Redressing the balance."

Danny exited the building, out into bright, searing sunshine. He blinked, waited for his sight to adjust, then paced around and back, within a 30-yard radius of the front entrance, trying to look inconspicuous, to blend in, as he scanned for likely suspects making phone calls. He saw a guy in a parked car, a skate-boarder, an obese businessman: all on the telephone, but none who fit the bill. Danny badly craved a cigarette. He slowly backed in the outer door, through the entrance into the lobby, still watching the street in front, cursing the inaccuracy of the tech team's triangulation…when they buzzed through again. He almost knocked the earpiece from his head in his eagerness. Danny said, "Yes… Where? Within the building or just outside. But that's…"

He whirled around and came face-to-face with a young man with shoulder-length hair. Nondescript features, not ugly but not especially memorable. The man smiled pleasantly—Danny reached for his piece.

"On the floor," he yelled. "*Now*! Down. Move it. Face down."

The man raised his hands in a gesture of submission, and lowered his body to the floor with exaggerated slowness, lying on his front.

Danny crouched down, saying, "That's it. Face down. Don't fucking move, kid. Just…stay…exactly…like…" He patted the man's sides, around his torso, and between his legs, ran a hand inside his pockets. Nothing—no phone, no weapon, nothing. Danny could feel his skin tingle with embarrassment; he suddenly felt very stupid. He holstered his gun and reached out a hand.

"Here. Grab my hand."

The guy hoisted himself up. Danny mumbled, "Sorry. Um…look, I'm really sorry. My mistake. Thought you were…"

The other man shrugged and smiled, then gestured to the door.

Danny said, "What? Yeah, yeah. Shit. Sorry. Yes, of course. You're free to go."

The long-haired man stepped briskly out the door. Danny stood there, frustrated and extremely tired. He looked to his left, where the woman at reception raised her eyebrows and smiled encouragingly. Danny weakly returned the smile.

He gently thumped a fist off his forehead and said to himself, "Fuck. *Fuck*."

Upstairs in the studio it was obvious that the interview was coming to an end, Wilde's voice rising in urgency and passion as he delivered a closing spiel: "…way past time to reclaim that term 'a real man.' The use of power defines the powerful. A real man isn't someone who's violent or misogynist, someone who drinks whiskey and smokes filter-less cigarettes and wrestles longhorn steer barehanded, or some other macho bullshit."

Bailey raised a hand and opened his mouth as if to protest the bad language, but Wilde just cut through him, even more vehemently: "Someone so fucking small and scared that they have to dump on others to compensate. A real man is brave and honest and feminine. And willing to do whatever needs to be done. You know that line from Ulrike Meinhof? 'Protest is when I say: this does not please me. Resistance is when I ensure that what doesn't please me occurs no more.' This is Karma TV ending transmission—for now."

The line went dead: a moment of nothingness, then the pips indicating a broken connection. Bailey sat there with a stupid look on his face. The on-duty floor manager belatedly realized that Bailey wasn't saying anything, that dead air was going out, ironically live, to millions of viewers. He issued hurried instructions to cut to a commercial break, before rushing in to confer with Bailey as to what should follow. Nobody, it seemed, had thought that far ahead.

To the side Murray Helmore turned to Cathy, rubbing his hands and smiling broadly. He said, "Well. I thought that went quite well, didn't you?"

And downstairs, Danny was jogging from the reception area to the next floor when he met Patrick, almost colliding with him as they each rounded a bend in the stairwell. Danny lifted his hands in mock submission and said, "Patrick. They let you leave your station?"

"Yeah, I...overheard one of those cops saying there was a commotion down at reception. Thought I'd check it out. I wasn't really doing much up there anyway."

"Well, it was a wasted trip, my friend. For all concerned. Another fucking false alarm."

Patrick tutted, a soft click at the back of his mouth. "That's... Shit. That's too bad."

Danny made as if to speak, then whirled around, slapping his hand off the white painted wall, grimacing, lips drawn back over pale gums. "Goddamit," he said. "He was *here*, Patrick, or somewhere nearby. I know it. And I let him go."

Patrick put his arm on Danny's shoulder. "Look, don't beat yourself up about it. You're doing your best, Danny."

"Yeah, I know, I'm just...really, seriously annoyed at myself. And at him, and at this whole fucking mess." He stopped, smiled, rolled his eyes to heaven. "Come on, let's go back upstairs."

They trotted up the stairs together, then the next flight, not speaking, each mulling things over. By the time they had reached the studio and were walking toward Bailey's desk, around which a knot of people stood talking, half an idea was germinating in Danny's mind.

He called over, "Mr. Bailey. Hello? Mr. Bailey? Do something for me, please: ring that number again."

Bailey looked at him dumbly.

Danny said, "Please. Ring it again. If Wilde is still somewhere in the vicinity, someone may hear the ring tone. I don't know. It's a long shot, but... Let's give it a go, okay?"

Bailey looked to the others clustered around him, as if seeking affirmation that he wasn't alone in thinking this cop was clutching at some pretty goddamn unlikely straws. None was forthcoming, so he shrugged and redialed. Silence—Bailey sighed, smugly and obviously—and then a phone was heard...and very close by. Surprised, people crept around, trying to locate its source.

Danny flapped his arms and hissed, "Shhh! *Quiet*, everyone, please. Just...quiet."

He listened, zoning in; then dashed to a corner, crawled under a desk...nothing there but a wastepaper basket. Danny pulled it out, upended it; the phone fell out. He lifted it and stared at the screen in bewilderment. It was still ringing, flashing yellow and vibrating slightly. He pressed connect and heard Bailey's heavy, astounded breathing on the other end.

Danny killed the connection and muttered, "How the hell...?"

He looked around—everyone was staring in amazement at the phone and at him. Cathy shook her head with the disordered but resigned expression of one who's just seen a ghost. Danny looked back at the phone, then shook his head and laughed.

He muttered, "Well, fuck me gently with a chainsaw. I give up. Either this guy is the invisible man or, or...or I don't know what. Or this is all a conspiracy and you're all involved, or something. Fuck...*me*."

Bailey whispered to Cathy, "What did I tell you, Cathy? About a conspiracy?"

She glared at him. Jesus, Jonathon. How obtuse can one man be? She would have slapped him across the head but there was a policeman in the room.

Lenny Bruce was on a roll, his voice carrying from a handheld stereo, positioned in the hallway, to the bathroom where Danny lay submerged in thick suds. This was one of Lenny's terrifying, wildly funny riffs on the Cuban Missile Crisis, the comedian's frantic delivery cranking up the still-palpable sense of hysteria, of mass dread. The room was dark save for a weak shaving light over the washbasin, and Danny settled his body deeper into the water, soothing his aching limbs and tired mind. He gingerly reached for the thin joint smoldering in a triangular ashtray and took a long, calming drag. The drug crawled through his system, ever so slowly, an almost imperceptible relaxing effect. Danny mumbled a song lyric, "How I love you, Mary-Jane", and thought, Could a cop really use a term like "Mary-Jane"? He might have to amend it, for personal purposes, to "How I love you, Schedule 1 controlled substance."

He smiled at his joke, easing into the water further and placing the joint to his lips, and then his phone rang. He scrambled for it, knocking the joint and ashtray to the ground, and pressed the button to connect.

"Danny Everard. Yes, James... What time? ...Okay. Did they give a cause of death? Alright. Thank you for calling, James. What...? Yeah, sure it changes matters. They're not just kidnappers anymore; they're killers. ...Okay, I'll talk to you then. G'night."

So Coronado was dead. Okay—that changed things. Turned them up another notch. Danny pushed the door ajar, dampening the sound of Lenny and his manic screams of delighted terror.

He thought for a moment and dialed straight through to Peter's voicemail.

"Peter—it's Danny. Don't reply to this message, I just... I wanna apologize for the other night, and for not calling like we arranged. I was, ah...caught up. Anyway, sorry again. I was an asshole, and I know it. Listen, I'm gonna be busy for a while. This case, it's... I'll call you when this is over, okay? ...I love you."

He hung up, let out a long groan, and submerged his head beneath the foam.

Life on Mars

Life imitating art...or is this something even better?

BY: JIMI NEILSEN, WRITER-AT-LARGE

It's one of the corniest clichés to bedevil this fine trade of ours, but you're just gonna have to bear with me as I use it again. Does life imitate art, or art imitate life, or both simultaneously? The question has long been passionately debated by students of modern culture, but it seems, now, we may have a winner.

Life imitating art? Hell, this is life *bettering* the damn thing.

What in the name of God is Nielsen rambling on about?, you're thinking right now. Well, unless you've been in suspended animation for the last little while, you will be aware of a certain

October issue

The connoisseur's guide to music

vigilante gang, plying their nefarious wares throughout New York and, at time of writing, still on the loose. You will also be aware that the gang has since made a televized interview with Network 4's Jonathon Bailey, in which they outlined their ideals and motives.

And you will assuredly, dear reader, be aware that a Pearl Jam lyric was found at the scene of their third crime, the abduction and killing of a local man of, shall we say, ill repute.

Still not making the connection? Okay – allow me: The 3W Gang, by their own admission, is somewhere to the radical side of Andrea Dworkin when it comes to gender and sexuality issues. These guys are kicking ass and taking names in the cause of a more equitable society, one which treats men and women, straight and gay, with the same respect. All well and good, you might say.

Now here's the kicker: The strident feminism and advocacy of gay rights? The lofty principles? The blurring of demarcation lines between masculine and feminine? The erudition and social awareness they bring to their work? (Jeez, my editor's gonna kill me for this. No, I am *not* defending their actions or the men themselves. Just trying to make a point.) And finally, the Pearl Jam lyric?

They all add up to one thing: this is *grunge made real*. You remember grunge, right? Early 1990s, mainly Seattle-based, sludgy guitars and introspective lyrics, plaid shirts, goatee

Pages 35–36

Life on Mars

beards?

Sure you do. Grunge took back loud guitars from the poodle-rock pin-up boys and gave it a heart, a soul, and a brain. It reconciled a love for heavy rock with a thoughtful, almost feminine nature. These guys totally rocked but weren't afraid to show their sensitive side.

Pearl Jam wrote songs about domestic abuse, sexual assault, society's maltreatment of the mentally ill. Stone Temple Pilots' *Sex Type Thing* addressed the issue of date rape.

Nirvana implored homophobes and other macho assholes not to buy their albums. Alice in Chains dug deeply and honestly into the black hole of drug addiction. Even contemporary bands with more obscure aesthetics, such as Helmet and Soundgarden, eschewed the old-style rock-star image of babes, booze and fast cars for cropped hair, college degrees, and ever-present frowns.

Most grunge bands were politically active, aligning themselves to a broad range of left-wing causes, including women's and homosexual rights campaigns. Lollapalooza, that era's annual travelling festival, combined music with information stalls on everything from organic food to registering for your vote. And this is without even mentioning the several mainly female bands of the time, such as Hole, L7, Sleater-Kinney, and Bikini Kill, who rocked just as hard and loud as their brethren.

It was all a long way from Axl Rose

October issue

The connoisseur's guide to music

thrusting his crotch into your face on MTV, and of course it couldn't, and didn't, last. Grunge was soon replaced by testosterone-fuelled frat-boy rock acts like Limp Bizkit and an array of pimp-wannabe gangsta rappers. *Plus ça change, plus c'est la même chose*, and all that.

But my, oh my, didn't someone learn their lesson well at the feet of Eddie, Kurt, Scott, Courtney, and the rest? Some little skater kids, maybe, delving into big bro's or big sis's record collection after all the hoop-la had died down and the music world had moved on. Precocious kids who should have been doing their homework, but were instead getting an alternative education from the music, lyrics, interviews, and attitude of their favorite grunge bands.

Wilde, Waters, and Whitman are not imitating art – they've learned its lessons and are applying them to life. And like those bands, these guys are fired-up, knowledgeable, and *angry as hell*.

When grunge's heyday passed, many people heaved a sigh of relief. Now we could get back to normality, they said, where rock music was made by real men, and feminism was for pussies and weirdo hippies. Others lamented the end of an era when ideas of maleness expanded and evolved into new and interesting directions. Most of us figured, either way, we'll be too old to give a damn by the time this thing comes around again.

Now, more than a decade-and-a-half later, grunge has finally made its triumphant return – just not in a form any of us had expected.

Pages 37–38

Chapter 10

Shootout

"THE fucking guy is *dead*, Paddy. He's dead, and we fucking killed him!"

Patrick gazed up at a poster of a kitschy 1950s sci-fi movie which hung on the wall of his parents' basement. He didn't want to think about Robert's words, not yet. He stared at the poster, taking in all its elements separately, then together. The garish, primary colors, so popular at that time; the chunky, comic book typeface used for the name of the movie; the pneumatic girl shrieking in the foreground, the granite-jawed hero turned toward the background; the alien monster lumbering toward them, looking every inch the cardboard cut-out it no doubt was. He'd enjoyed that movie, enjoyed the cheap ironic thrills of its sheer awfulness, when he'd watched it during a sci-fi festival in a seamy little theater in LA, three or four years back. And of course, he'd had to buy the poster afterward. A little memento of the event; something to mark the moment.

He sat on a beanbag, against the wall, underneath a shelf heaving with electronic gizmos, stacks of CDs, several books. Robert Eustace—AKA Waters, AKA the long-haired guy encountered by Danny at the TV studios—sat at a computer desk. He was crying. The tears rolled down his pale, soft face as he slugged back a beer and pulled at clumps of his sandy hair. On the ground next to Patrick sat a huge, black-haired man, stubbled and bear-like, a biker sort: Whitman, AKA Alessandro "Sandro" Tomassi. His face was blank of expression. He stared at the ground, at his thick-soled black boots.

Patrick rested his head in his hands and said quietly, "*We* didn't kill him, Robert; I killed him. I'll take the responsibility for it."

Robert swallowed more beer, choking back his sobs. He said, "It doesn't matter who takes the fall, Paddy. The pimp is dead, and this whole thing has gotten out of control. We fucking *said* there'd be no killing. No one was supposed to die!"

Sandro stood and moved across, putting a burly arm around

Robert. He didn't say anything. He turned and raised his eyebrows to Patrick who looked toward the ceiling, anguish on his face. There was the camouflage netting, pinioned to the four corners, a gift from Lillian some years previously: "LA LUCHA CONTINÚA." She'd always teased him about his admiration of Che Guevara.

"There you go, sweet-pea," she'd said. "My little revolutionary. Some inspiration for your future."

Patrick had laughed and thrown the banner over her, and they'd fallen together to the floor of his room. He smiled and remembered how Lillian used to bundle her hair up in a loose bun, how graceful it made her neck look. She was a fine woman.

"LA LUCHA CONTINÚA." The struggle continues. Good enough.

Patrick stood, determined. He said, "I'm sorry, Robert. You don't know how sorry I am. It wasn't meant to happen, but it did. I took a human life, and I'll have to live with that for the rest of my time here. But we can't let that stop us. We're near the end now. This wasn't something that could have gone on indefinitely. We're just beginning the work, we're starting the chain-reaction. And now we're near the end of our part and we have to make a final statement. Will you make it with us?"

Robert was still crying; he took another drink and burbled, "Guy is... This fucking Coronado is *dead*, man. I can't get my head around this, I can't..."

They let him talk himself out. There was silence for a few moments. Patrick crouched down beside Robert and whispered, "Will you do this one last thing? Robert?"

Robert hesitated, shaking his head angrily; then he lifted his bloodshot eyes to Patrick's and nodded.

No. It just didn't fit right.

He couldn't, if pressed, have said exactly what was hinky about that interview with Wilde, but it was something. Danny had always trusted his instinct, despite a proud reliance on rationality and rigorous mental processes to understand events. He sat in his office and shook his head, and he *knew*: something about the voice didn't fit. He pushed play on an audio recording of the interview.

Wilde was saying, "For a group of men to kick another to death because of his sexuality is unacceptable…" He pressed fast-forward, the voice squeaking like a hyperactive mechanical mouse, then pushed the play button again: "…man is brave and honest and feminine. And willing to do whatever needs to be done…"

Danny sat up sharply. "There. The voice. A different speaker. It's a different fucking speaker!"

He pressed stop, stood up, and began pacing the floor, mumbling to himself, running it through, playing the mental riff. "Okay. Think this through logically, Everard. You went down to the lobby. You walked around. You saw…nothing much. You stepped back inside. You turned… No—the tech team called you: they'd located the signal. Then you turned, and bumped into that guy…"

He absentmindedly lit a cigarette and stood there for a moment, not smoking it. A thin wisp of smoke drifted past his eye line and something clicked in his mind. Now *go*. He opened the door just as another detective, an overweight, red-faced man, stuck his head in and said, "Daniel-san. We're all going getting some early supper; wanna come with?"

Danny shoved the cigarette into his hand. "Sorry, Jonesy. Somewhere I gotta be. Finish that for me, would you?"

He stepped into the corridor and walked briskly away. Jones called after him: "Thanks, Everard. I'd appreciate it even more if I actually smoked and it wasn't totally fuckin' illegal in here, but hey…"

Danny sprinted into the Network 4 building, flashing his badge at the receptionist and pointing upward. He said, "Cathy

Morrissey? Is she here?"

Jennifer replied, "No, I think she's gone home for the evening, sir. Would you like me to...?"

"No, no, it's fine. I'm just going to her office, okay?"

Jennifer said, with her customary indifference, "Sure thing."

Danny debated taking the elevator before sprinting the three flights to Cathy's office. He could feel it, the illumination of his nerve ends, the whole body beginning to spark. He knew he was closing in. He ran down the brightly lit corridor and entered her office, closing the door behind him. He moved to the desk, tossing around the papers and bits of detritus scattered there, then scanned the walls frantically. Keep it cool, Danny boy. Much haste means less speed, and all that. Memos, postcards, silly signs... And there, in the corner, partly hidden, a photograph of Patrick and Cathy at a party: arms around each other, and beside Cathy...the long-haired guy from the lobby. Closer all the time.

Danny pulled the photo down and dialed on his cell phone: "Cathy? It's Danny Everard. Cathy, I'm in your office and there's something really important I have to ask you. Are you ready? You have a photo on your wall—small, a snapshot with a disposable camera—it's of you, and Patrick, and a third man... Yeah, it's a party of some kind... Yeah. I need to know his name... *Think*, Cathy... Robert. Is that all you remember? Robert something; a friend of Patrick. Alright. A friend of Patrick..."

He closed his eyes, thinking of a possible chronology, imagining...

Visualizing Patrick leaving the studio immediately after him; going downstairs by a different route; passing Robert in the lobby and discreetly collecting the phone; slipping into a quiet corner to finish the interview; meeting Danny on the stairs and returning to the studio with him; dropping the phone into the wastepaper basket.

It's possible. To hell with that, it's *more* than possible. It's likely. That's what happened. He was startled by Cathy's voice on the other end of the line, sounding a million miles away but simultaneously up close.

Danny snapped back to reality and said, "What...? Yeah, I'm still here. Listen, thanks, Cathy—you've been more than helpful. Do you have Patrick's home address? Ask at reception, okay. ...I can't right now. I'll explain it later, I promise. Please—trust me. Thank you." He hung up and spun around, energized and infuriated. "Fuck it! I *had* him. I had him yesterday and the day before and the day before that." Danny looked at the photo again. "I had you, Patrick. I had you that night, and I had you yesterday, and I let you go, kiddo." A pause. "Why did you play that game yesterday? Why take risks like that? Did you want to be caught, Patrick?"

He smiled bitterly. "You're about to be."

Danny crumpled the photo into his pocket and moved.

The evening was getting chilly, underneath a blue-black sky, as hip-hop star Eye Dog trotted down the steps to the street in front of his Midtown recording studio. *His* recording studio—his own, not two blocks from Radio City Music Hall, bought with the proceeds of his 25 million record sales. Eye Dog was king of the hill now, and the money was rolling in. The studio, the cars, the mansion, the jewelry, the women queuing up to fuck him and the men to pay him respect. If his old acquaintances could only see him now—his parents, his teachers, rival rappers from the old days, that evil bitch he'd called his wife for a brief spell, those pussy journalists who'd described him as an ignorant thug, a cheap punk. Suck on that, you faggot fucks.

He felt good about life right then, and good about that recording session. The new tracks were shit hot. Jelly Skell and Dee-Monn were still inside, sipping cognac and discussing Jelly's new helicopter. Man, a fucking helicopter! The thought of that skinny fool parading around in a helicopter made Eye Dog laugh. He'd have to find out the price of one of those things for himself.

His limo pulled up as he hit the curb, right on cue, and the back door popped open. Eye Dog sat in and lowered his trademark diamond-encrusted monocle from his eye. Fucking thing looked good but it got pretty uncomfortable after a while.

He hit the driver intercom: "Right on time as usual, Donner. Turn up the heating back here, would you, man? Pretty damn cold outside."

The door locks snapped down and Eye Dog could see the driver, through the smoked glass partition, lift his head and fix on a balaclava. He frowned and said, "What is this shit? Donner? Is that you?"

The partition slid down smoothly. The driver turned to Eye Dog, pointing a gun.

He said, "Donner is a goner. And so are you."

A tranquilizer dart in the neck knocked Eye Dog out in less than five seconds.

A regular, well-kept house on a quiet street. Lace curtains in the windows and pot plants by the front door. An elaborate brass knocker. Beautifully detailed stained glass in a semi-circle over the door. Columbia University nearby, elegant brownstones, leaves turning to red and gold, a discreet air of affluence. So this is the place.

Danny approached cautiously. He pulled his gun, chambered it, crept up the steps. He listened; no sound from within. In fact, no sounds at all—this really was the definition of a sleepy residential area. Danny pulled out his radio and hesitated. He decided not to call it in; he'd play it out a little first, try and minimize any trouble. He was scared: not for himself, but of how Patrick would react if cornered. A part of him was already regretting it, but he had decided to try and reason with the guy, talk him into coming quietly. It wasn't that he owed that much to Patrick, or maybe it was; he didn't fucking know anymore.

He pushed against the door—locked. Danny leaned his foot

back for leverage, and hesitated again: he had no warrant. Legally, he had no right to enter this building without the owner's permission. But he had probable cause, right? His ass was fried if this went wrong; worse, Patrick could walk on a technicality. Danny juggled the two contentions in his head, weighing one against the other, gamble against reward. He was on the trail of a known and dangerous criminal; it would be an abdication of responsibility to allow anything further to develop. But if he could prove that, then get a warrant. But how fast could he rouse a judge to sign one?

No more buts. He lifted his leg again and kicked hard.

Danny moved, carefully but swiftly, through the house— empty. He'd known it would be. Inside, it was as normal and blandly middle-class as its façade. Expensive, tasteful rugs, classic furniture, family pictures and mahogany bookshelves; he was almost starting to doubt his own convictions. He reached the basement, the door of which was padlocked. Danny took a step back, fired, snapping the metal. He knocked off the lock with the gun-butt and stepped inside...

And all his fears were confirmed: Patrick was Wilde. Even though he had been expecting this, he still found it baffling, almost unthinkable. But the evidence was undeniable. He rifled through drawers and desktops, mentally catalogued the film and audio equipment, registered the sort of books Patrick had been reading. Danny joggled the computer mouse and the screen came to bright life with a "shh" sound. He opened Internet Explorer and flicked through the History option, noting websites Patrick had visited: pages popped up with information on weaponry, technology, cutting-edge equipment. Why hadn't he deleted the History? Folders on the computer desktop, with essays on gender, homophobia, societal trends, dozens of them.

Danny sat on a beanbag in the corner, shaking his head, unsure what to do now, how to explain himself. I mistakenly thought I saw Broder enter the building. I received a tip-off from a concerned neighbor, a local busybody. The door was busted open when I got here.

He laughed at that one, but still wasn't sure what he was going to say as he moved to the phone on Patrick's desk and dialed Harte's number. It went straight to his answering machine: "You're through to James Harte's voicemail. I'm sorry, I can't take your call right now. You know what to do after the beep, so...do it after the beep."

Danny hung up without leaving a message. He noticed Patrick's university scrolls on the wall: a bachelor's degree in English literature, a master's in film and TV production. Photos dotted the walls, taken at wide intervals as evidenced by the changing hairstyles and clothes. Some of them had hand-written titles affixed beneath. A younger Patrick and this guy Robert: "Me and Rob after second-year exams." Patrick as a child with a much larger, dark-haired boy: "Sandro and me start elementary school."

Danny murmured, "Ha. Mr. Whitman, I presume."

Another photo, of all three this time, arms around each other's shoulders and holding beers: "The three amigos in Mexico, 2007. Too much to drink!" A few pictures of Patrick and different girls embracing, smiling happily at the camera: "Lillian and me touring BC"; "Courtney's graduation party"; "Sarah lazing in the bath." Danny scanned the bookshelves—a big variety of writers, styles, genres—and pulled one out at random. It was a book of twentieth century poetry, inscribed, "To Paddy, the poet of the family. Congratulations on finishing school, and never lose your love of language. From Mom, Dad, Marie, and the two dogs."

Eventually, reluctantly, he hit the speaker button on Patrick's phone and tapped in a number. A voice rang out: "Dispatch."

"Detective Sergeant Danny Everard, Midtown South Precinct. I want to issue a city-wide APB for the arrest of young white male Patrick Broder—that's B-R-O-D-E-R, Patrick, AKA Wilde.

Blond hair, slim build, about six feet tall. And associates: young white male Robert no-known-second-name, AKA Waters. Sandy-colored hair, slim build, five-eight to five-nine. And Sandro—that's short for Alessandro, I'm guessing, no-known-second name, AKA…"

"Uh, Detective?"

"Yes?"

"Well, sir, those men are, um…well, they're on TV."

Danny frowned. "What do you mean, 'on TV'?"

"I mean they're on TV, sir. Right now. They're on Network 4 for the last five minutes. I thought everyone knew this…"

"What the hell are you…?"

Danny turned on the TV and flicked through to Network 4. The broad face and muscular upper torso of a young black man glared at a point behind the camera. The man looked a little scared but also surly, uncooperative, defiant. His face was vaguely familiar to Danny—a rapper or something, he wasn't sure. Then he heard Patrick's voice off-screen—not Wilde this time, but Patrick, transparent and uncovered—saying to the man, "…don't hear any remorse in your voice, fuck-stick. You're not getting out of here until I hear some remorse. And truth."

Danny dashed out the door without switching off the set. The dispatcher called out, his voice sounding somehow forlorn: "Uh…sir? Hello, Detective? Are you there, Detective?"

Bobby and Johnny had both worked night security at Network 4 for more years than they cared to remember. It wasn't exactly the dream job either had imagined for themselves in school, but what the hey—the pay was good and the work was easy. The job basically involved sitting on your fat ass for eight hours, five nights a week, and keeping an eye on things. They had a bank of CCTV screens in their small office, toward the rear of the building, and every 30 minutes one of them would make the perfunctory rounds. The greatest excitement you could expect would be rousting the odd wino who was looking for a warm place to sleep. Most of the time the work comprised respectfully tipping your cap to whatever big-shot was coming in or going out. Those souped-up assholes who worked the day shift would never stick the boredom, though. *Those* clowns thought they were in the marines or something. Bobby and Johnny just laughed at them behind their backs.

Now Bobby sat in the booth, feet up on the bank of screens, stretching his hands behind his head. Johnny, standing beside him, said, "So what did you say you wanted again?"

"I said I wanted a Snickers, a bottle of orange juice, and 20 Luckies. And get me a magazine too. A nudie. I'm bored stiff here."

Johnny chuckled. "Well, you'll be bored stiffer when you read one of those. Whaddya want? *Hustler*? *Asian Babes*?"

"*No*. God, no. Just get me, like, a *Playboy* or something. Nothing too hardcore. I like my filth to be relatively clean, if you follow me."

They both laughed, and Johnny said, "Bobby, Bobby, Bobby… you're just too bad, Bobby…"

Some 30 feet away a side-door hushed open and the 3W Gang, dressed in tuxedos but without their balaclavas, quietly slipped into the building. Patrick and Sandro dragged a drugged, sluggish Eye Dog between them. Robert carefully closed the door. Johnny and Bobby continued their conversation.

They quickly pulled Eye Dog up little-used maintenance stairwells, then pushed him through a door and along a short corridor, finally entering the cramped confines of Studio Two. Sandro bolted the door through which they'd entered, one of two access points. Robert stood still, hesitant. Patrick, placing Eye Dog into the presenter's chair behind a desk, stopped and looked at Robert.

He said, "Come *on*, Rob. The other door."

"Paddy, man. I don't know about this…"

"You don't know what? Secure the other fucking door, Rob."

Robert hesitated again, then breathed heavily and moved to the far corner, padlocking the fire exit. Sandro stripped Eye Dog of his coat and shirt, down to a white vest, and bound him with dull-silver duct tape, arms and head, into the presenter's chair behind a desk. He fixed a camera onto the man's face.

Robert took a step forward and blurted out, "Listen, I've got a bad goddamn feeling. This is… What are we doing here, dude?"

"Jesus Christ, Robert. Not now," Patrick said. "I don't have time for this now."

"Look, I'm with you, man. You know that. But this, it's…I don't know…"

Patrick looked at him, angry, strain showing in his ragged eyes. He barked, "*What*? What is the matter? Come on, tell me."

Robert didn't respond. Patrick continued, "You have a problem, say so. What is it? What's the problem!?"

Still no answer. Sandro stepped between them, saying, "It's okay, Paddy. Everything's cool." He turned to Robert. "Right, little man?"

Robert nodded and spoke wearily. "Right, Sandro."

"No problem," Patrick said. "Good."

Sandro moved away, toward the control room, as Robert fixed on his balaclava. Eye Dog was beginning to return to consciousness, slowly, as Patrick slipped on his hood and stepped in front of the camera. He turned to Robert and said quietly, "Rob—it's okay. I told you. Everything will go as it should."

Robert swallowed hard and nodded. Patrick steadied himself and looked up to Sandro who gave him the A-OK sign, as Robert stood nervously by, holding a gun, a bag at his feet. A red "Recording" light blinked on—the 3W Gang had now patched into the main transmission feed and were going out live. Television viewers across New York were annoyed, then perplexed, as their reception momentarily went fuzzy, before clearing to reveal a masked man half-filling their screens. He cleared his throat and smiled.

Patrick said, in his own voice, "Good evening, citizens, and welcome once more to Karma TV. I must apologize in advance for the roughshod nature of tonight's production—we're going out live, so you can expect one or two...minor mishaps. But don't let that put you off, because we have a very, *very* special guest tonight. Please, a warm, heartfelt welcome for rap sensation...Eye Dog."

He stepped aside to reveal their captive, now fully awake and wondering just what the hell this was all about.

Patrick said, "We've brought you some real scumbags so far, folks, but tonight we thought it might be nice to present a famous face. A sort of...*celebrity* scumbag, if you will. Why not tell us a little about yourself, Eye Dog? Or may I call you Eye?"

"Wha-? What the fuck is happening here? Is this a set-up? Yeah. This is a set-up. Right, punk? You're gonna pull off that stupid mask any second and..."

Patrick sighed theatrically. "It's not a mask, Eye Dog; it's a balaclava. Named for a battle in the Crimean War, I believe. And no, it's not a set-up, either. Watch." He pulled a gun from inside his jacket and started aiming it, back and forth, with one eye closed. "Hmm...where, oh where, to fire?"

Then he shot a hole in the presenter's chair, about an inch below Eye Dog's left ear. The rapper jumped, shocked, started yelling, "Aargh! Jesus Christ! What are you *doing*!?"

"What am I doing? Something that should have been done a long time ago, Mr. Big-time Fucking Hip-Hop Star. At the risk of laboring a musical theme, Eye Dog, it's time for *you* to pay the piper."

By the time Danny screeched his car to a halt across the street from the Network 4 building, the forces of law and order had begun amassing outside. Squad cars formed a perimeter of steel and flashing blue lights. Men in long overcoats spoke with urgency into radios. A SWAT team gathered in front of the main entrance, about a dozen of them, muscular men in bulky black jackets and reinforced helmets, throat mikes and earpieces, powerful submachine-guns held at ease in both hands. And, of course, the TV cameras were already setting up equipment and breathlessly reporting back to studio.

Danny jogged forward but was stopped ten yards from the front door by the SWAT team leader, a huge man with a bristling moustache. He said, "Whoa. Cool your heels right there, pal."

Danny flashed his badge and said, "Detective Sergeant Everard. You have to let me through."

The man shook his head nonchalantly. "Uh-uh. Nothin' doin'. Nobody goes in or out until the Chief okays it. Alright? That's a direct order from the man himself."

Danny couldn't believe this shit. Every cop's worst bureaucratic nightmare made flesh. He pleaded, "I'm handling this case, for Christ's sake. Working under Captain James Harte of the 14th Precinct. I know this man, I can talk with him, please. Stop being so fucking obtuse."

The SWAT leader held up his hand. "Stop. Stop talking to me. I'm following my orders, alright? Take it up with your Captain Jonathan Harte if you want."

Danny stepped back, infuriated. He was debating whether or not to call James when he heard Cathy. He turned and saw her, struggling to break through an NYPD cordon.

Cathy shouted, "Danny! Over here! Danny!"

He rushed over and, taking her hands, moved them back through the cordon, away from the front door. They stopped under the spreading boughs of a tree, oddly menacing in the flickering glow of the vehicles' lights.

"Cathy. What are you doing here?" Danny said. "You don't wanna..."

"Is it true, Danny? Someone said they'd...kidnapped a movie

star, or something… That they've got him holed up inside our building, right now…"

"Shh. Yes, it's true. He's got him in one of the studios. I couldn't stop him, I only found out today…"

Cathy frowned, puzzled. "Couldn't stop who? Who's 'he'? …Danny?"

Danny made to speak, then stopped himself. He sighed heavily and looked away.

"What? Talk to me, Danny. Who… Wait a minute. It's not…"

He looked at her and nodded.

Cathy said, quietly, "Patrick? You think… No. Nooo." She laughed nervously. "You must be mistaken, Detective. Patrick couldn't… Are you serious?"

"I'm serious, Cathy. Patrick is in there right now, with his two friends and some…guy, a rap star I think…"

"Wait. Robert? Is he involved, too? Oh my God, Danny. This is *insane*." She went silent, thinking, sucking on the inside of her cheek. "The leaks. The videotape leaked to other studios. No. I can't *believe* this. This is nuts…"

Danny took her in a bear hug and said, "I know. I know. It *is* crazy, you're right." He pushed them apart and looked into her eyes. "Listen—I'm gonna do my best here. I can't promise anything…" He gestured to the forces ranked around them. "…but I'll do my best. Okay? Patrick will be alright. Trust me?"

She nodded and whispered, "Thank you."

Eye Dog was beginning to feel a little uncomfortable. Sure, he could take this punk-ass bitch one to one, any time; he could slap his ass all the way from here to Canada. But he wasn't so sure about the other guy, the big one up high in the control room: he looked like a man who knew how to take care of himself. And besides, the punk-ass bitch was holding a gun by his side, and Eye Dog's arms were tied down anyway.

Patrick leaned over him, and Eye Dog looked away, a curl on

his lip. Don't show any fear. *You* are the fucking boss of this situation. You didn't come up through the ghetto just to get pushed around by some sissy white boy who thinks he's Steven fuckin' Seagal. Eye Dog looked back—the guy was still staring at him.

He said, "What? What you staring at me like that for?"

Patrick replied, "I'm waiting, Eye Dog. And so are all the viewers at home. We're waiting for your confession."

"My what? You've gotta be fucking kidding, right?" Then he remembered the gun, and thought, Play it cool, Dog. Do what he says. Let him get comfortable. "No. Okay. You're not kidding. That's cool, man. Whatever you want."

"Well, get to it, then. This silence is hemorrhaging viewers; our corporate sponsors will not be pleased."

Eye Dog shrugged, as much as anyone in his position could, and said, "Yeah, sure. My confession about what? Yo, I'm not being funny, man. I don't know what you're talking about. Seriously."

Patrick stood back, away from the desk. "Alright. Let me refresh your memory and fill in some of the background blanks for the good folks in TV land." He addressed the camera. "Mr. Dog, ladies and gentlemen, has a particularly—how shall I phrase this?—*unpleasant* attitude toward the fairer sex. And toward homosexuals. Oh, and as it happens, Jews and Koreans, too, which I think shows commendable inclusiveness."

He turned and glared at Eye Dog; Eye Dog glared back.

Patrick went on, "Just give me a minute...ah, yes." He raised a finger. "This is from the charmingly titled album, *Bitch on a Leash*: 'Suck that dick, bitch, suck it, ho; I know you wanna suck it cuz that's all that you good fo'.'" Patrick winced. "God, that *grammar*. Or how about this, from the—Christ almighty—award-winning album, *FAF*, or *Fuck All Faggots*: 'On ya hands and knees, faggot, do what I please, faggot; Glock up yo' ass and the trigger I squeeze, faggot.' Mm. Yummy. Makes me feel all warm inside."

He turned back to Eye Dog. "Yeah—I've heard some of your fucking records. Mediocre work, by the way."

Eye Dog stared at the ceiling. Patrick said, "Out of curiosity, do you realize the irony of a homophobe writing about, quote-unquote, 'fucking faggots'? Does that register with you, at all?"

The rapper looked back at him and said, "Man, what are you talking about? Fuckin' *irony*. Listen, let me outta this chair."

Patrick raised the gun and strode forward to within three feet of Eye Dog. He said, "No, *you* listen. I don't hear any remorse in your voice, fuck-stick. You're not getting out of here until I hear some remorse. And truth."

"*Truth*?" Eye Dog laughed. "What do you know about truth, motherfucker? There in your fancy-dress costume. In a mask. And you're askin' me about truth?"

"Ah. Classic justificatory behavior. 'You're just the same as me', et cetera, et cetera." He leaned forward and squeezed Eye Dog's left ear lobe, painfully, twisting the man's head upward. "We're not the fucking same. You hear me? I am *not* the same as you. Now talk."

He released the ear and turned away, and Eye Dog squirmed, trying not to show his discomfort. That had *hurt*. He slyly eyeballed the man in the mask and then it dawned: these are the guys all the news shows had been talking about. The vigilantes. The terrorists. The masked fucking avengers. He swallowed hard and thought, This could get serious.

"Man, don't kill me," Eye Dog exclaimed. "Alright? I haven't done shit, so just…don't kill me."

Patrick turned to face him. "Oh, but you *have*, Mr. Dog. And you know you have."

"Yo, *fuck* you. I didn't… What are you talking about?"

Patrick sighed. He shifted the balaclava back and forth on the crown of his head a few times. He placed both hands on the desk, the gun in one, fingers arched and tensed on the other, and said, "You've made a fortune out of this, this, woman-hating *shit* you peddle. This disgusting linguistic violence, dressed up as music. 'Women are bitches. Homosexuals are scum. Be like me. Be a fucking barbarian in gaudy jewelry. Be a *man!*'" Patrick laughed. "Christ. 'Be a man.' And you've gotten rich on this shit, baby. This incitement to hatred, more or less. But you know the best thing of all? I don't think you even believe any of it, anyway. It's all just a means of making the green, right? Man, the cynicism of *that*."

Eye Dog squirmed against his binds, his broad shoulders flexing, rippling under his skin. His expression was angry but also subdued. He said, "What's cynical about it? I'm just telling it like it is, man. Just keeping it real. You said you wanted truth; well, there it is."

Patrick shook his head. Robert stood ten feet away, scratching behind his ear, a nervous tic. Patrick turned back to the rapper and said, "No. No, I'm afraid that's bullshit. 'Keeping it real.' How fucking *lazy*. You're gonna have to come up with something better than that."

There was silence again, ten, 15 seconds of nothing, carrying from the studio mikes to the transmission tower to hundreds of thousands of TV sets. Patrick started tapping his index finger on the desk. He said, "Tick, tick, tick." No response. Then he slammed the desk with the side of his gun, hard: "I *said* tick, tick, tick!"

Eye Dog spat back, "Okay! You're right. Happy now? Feel all good about yourself? Yeah, I rap about bitches and faggots. All that. And you know why? 'Cause that's what the people want. Or can't you see that behind your mask, you self-righteous bastard? They don't want your pussy-ass, hold-hands, let's-all-be-friends shit. They want what *I* give 'em. They want the violence and sex and glamour I provide."

"Ha! Glamor? I'm sorry, am I confusing you with someone else?"

"Yeah, glamor. The life I lead, most guys'd kill for a sniff of that. Limos and money and bitches crawlin' all over you? Sure, they'd kill for that. A pussy like you might not, but that ain't my problem."

Patrick flipped the gun around in his hand, catching it by the barrel, and cracked Eye Dog on the top of the head with the butt. He grimaced and yelped, "Mother*fucker*! I'm bleedin' here! ...Do that again and I will cut you open."

"I already warned you about your intemperate language, Eye Dog. So cool it with the swearing, there's a good fellow."

Eye Dog shook his head, disbelieving, seething, and a little scared, as a trickle of blood made its dark way down his face. Patrick stood in silence for a moment, his hand to his face.

He spoke without looking at the other man: "Do you ever consider the consequences of what you do? Not just the ethical rights and wrongs of it, but the actual, concrete effects it has on people. On the whole of society. Do you think about that, or is it all just something you do? You go through life and do what you do and fuck the consequences." He faced Eye Dog again. "What I want to know is: is that all there is to it?"

Danny could feel the escalation in tension outside, incremental and almost tangible. The troops were getting restless, but nothing had been decided yet. Everyone remained in position, limbs starting to get stiff, the initial adrenaline rush subsiding, replaced with a bored sort of anxiety. He did not have a good feeling about any of it as he and Cathy stood just outside the cordon around the building.

He said, "Come *on*. What's taking them so long? Fuck it. This is all going bad. Cathy, is there another way in? A service entrance or something."

She nodded, worry etched on her face. "Yeah. We can get in by the underground parking lot. Half a block away. There's an old gate they don't use any more. It's padlocked."

Danny patted his gun in its holster and smiled: "I've got a key." He wasn't sure if he really found that funny or not.

"From there it's a pretty straight run up to Studio 2. That's most likely where Patrick is at. It'd make sense to bring him there."

Danny took her hand and said, "If only the rest of this made as much. C'mon."

"What really slays me about guys like you, Eye Dog, is how fucking indulged you are by society. You know, the way people laugh and raise their eyebrows at yet more tales of antisocial behavior from you and your ilk. The latest controversial lyric or outrageous comment. The latest story—never proven, of course—of naïve young girls at parties, getting passed around like a fucking joint between the lot of you."

Patrick was walking back and forth in front of Eye Dog, intermittently addressing him and the camera. He continued, "Like it's okay, it's acceptable, because hey!—they're superstars. Rap stars, rock stars, cock stars, it's all a big joke. Am I right?"

Eye Dog stayed silent and looked at the desk.

Patrick said, "Yeah, you know I'm right, you miserable fucking weasel. You know that if a busman or doctor or a fucking sheepherder got up to the same shit as you do, it's a goddamn court case they'd be looking at." He stopped and laughed to himself for a moment. "'The sexually sadistic sheepherder. He loves his sheepdog but hates all bitches.' Ha! What a concept. But for you, Eye Dog, it's wine and candy all the way. Increased record sales, a sprinkling of outlaw glamor, and of course, enough naïve young girls attending enough wild parties. Ah— ain't life grand?"

Eye Dog felt tired now. His eyes were dry and sore from the studio lights, his mouth felt like it had been rubbed with sandpaper, and this vigilante was starting to freak him out. He needed a shower and a drink. He needed to get out of this chair. He could hardly hear what the guy was saying any more, just words flowing from the mouth to his ears to his brain and back out again. What did this motherfucker *want* from him?

Eye Dog squinted up at Patrick and said wearily, "I don't... I never did nothing like that, man. Girls at parties. Swear to God..."

Finally, it was all starting to kick off outside. The SWAT team leader had received his orders, direct to his earpiece from the Big Cheese himself; had repeated them back, slowly, distinctly, and received confirmation. He prided himself on his ability to reduce fuck-ups and confusion to the bare minimum.

He stepped into the semi-circle formed by his men and, holding his submachine-gun high, delivered a final briefing: "Alright, my little treasures. We go in in 30 seconds. Gonzalez, take that goddamn chewing gum out of your stupid mouth. Now: although we're not sure how well armed they might be, there's only three of these assholes, so it shouldn't be a problem. And the rapper *must* be unharmed, guys. Got that? Not a fucking scratch. This fella's got important friends. Okay. On my signal."

It was obvious to Robert, as he shuffled from foot to foot, balancing his weight on one heel, then the next, trying to ignore the acid discomfort beginning to settle in his legs, that Patrick was losing his patience. It was like the Coronado thing all over again; the man strapped to the chair was being unresponsive, staring up at Patrick sullenly, the silence interspersed by the odd, aggressive declamation. What the courts might term a "hostile witness."

Patrick covered his microphone with his free hand and leaned in close, his breath tickling Eye Dog's ear. He whispered, "I know about Ladice Jones. I *know*. What you and your two friends did to her in that beach-house. How your lawyers covered it up because you're too much of a 'valuable asset.' That girl wasn't worth shit to you or them. Well, understand something: *you're* not worth shit to me. Understand? I will tear you apart. I don't care anymore."

Eye Dog flinched, there in the eyes, struggling to control his emotions, to look away or not look away, to appear appalled and wounded and innocent, and then Patrick did know.

He stood tall again, clutching the gun tightly, and declared loudly, "We tolerate this crap all the time because it's someone famous involved. We make jokes about the sort of thing sick fucks like you get up to. 'That's rock 'n' roll.' Well, the laughter stops here, godammit. You hear me, Eye Dog!?"

No reply. Patrick slapped Eye Dog with the back of his left hand, drawing blood. He shouted, "Look at me, damn you! I want to hear you say it, Eye Dog. I want you to confess what a nasty fucking piece of work you really are. In front of everyone watching. I want them to know what I know, you scumbag. Now confess. *Everything*."

Still no reply, and by now Eye Dog looked almost too scared to talk. Patrick leaped onto the desk, springing up there in one swift, fluid movement, squatting like a meditative monk and waving the gun in the air. "Tell the people, you son of a bitch. Now."

Eye Dog started spluttering, words falling over themselves in their anxiety to leave his mouth. All his brash courage, that learned bravado he'd assimilated growing up on tough streets, had dissolved. All he knew was this: he was tied to a chair and there was a crazy man pointing a gun in his face.

Patrick said, "Alright, fuck this", and jammed the gun into Eye Dog's mouth. The nauseating scrape of the barrel on his teeth was audible. The rapper grimaced, a dirty metal taste in his mouth, and tried to pull his head away. He could feel greasy streaks of sweat along his temples, down his neck and back. His eyes opened wide in fright and he began shaking his head "no", these tiny, furious movements. He heard himself moan and thought he was about to wet himself.

Patrick yelled, "*Tell* them! Or I swear to God…"

Robert took a step forward, alarmed. He shouted, "No!"

"Stay back, Rob," Patrick said, an eerie calm in his voice. "Tell them, Eye Dog. Tell everyone what a slimy little shit you are."

Robert remained there, paralyzed. By now even Sandro looked alarmed, standing up in the control room and removing his earphones, peering down. Patrick knocked off the safety, a thick, muted click, and Robert gasped. And then Cathy appeared at the small frosted window in the studio door, Danny immediately behind her. Patrick saw her, out of the corner of his eye, just a flash on his peripheral vision. He looked away and realized what he'd seen and looked again and there she was, looking at him quizzically. He pulled the gun from Eye Dog's mouth.

Cathy tilted her head and frowned. Through the glass they could see her mouth the word: "Patrick...?"

Patrick lowered the gun to his side. He rose to a standing position and said, "Cathy—go back...", and was whipped backward by the force of a bullet passing through his shoulder. The movie buff in him would have appreciated what happened next: like a scene from a John Woo flick. The slam-bang of hot metal tearing through his flesh, its momentum jerking him up and around. Then zoom back along the trajectory of the bullet, where smoke rose from the barrel of a SWAT team member's gun and glass fell slowly to the ground. Then cut to the slo-mo shot of Cathy and Danny, who had been roughly shoved aside, falling to the ground together. Then back to the first person point-of-view: Patrick turning slowly for a moment, a drunken ballerina, flailing and incapable, and crashing off the desk to the ground. And then, finally, the fade out, to blissful black...

Patrick lay on the floor, stunned and wounded. He knew his shoulder was in pain, but he couldn't feel it quite yet. The mind protecting the body for as long as it can. Time seemed to slow down, to a measured, lazy throb. He was acutely aware of his own labored breathing, and could distantly hear sounds, as though coming to him through walls of glass: Danny yelling at the SWAT team to stop as they battered at the door; Robert calling to Sandro to come down from the control room; Eye Dog screaming, all pretence at being a tough guy utterly vanished.

Then, for an instant, the flashback: the movie resumed in Patrick's mind as he saw himself, sitting on a beach in summertime, reading in the warm breeze. The wind made the long grass dance and flicked the pages of his book. He was young, 14 or 15, brightly blond and handsome, poring over the words and then smiling up at someone standing above him, casting a strong shadow in the burnished-yellow sunshine...

And now, the soundtrack: the sweet, elegiac strains of Percy Faith's *Theme from a Summer Place* started to play in his head, the jaunty strings leading in, the gorgeous sweep of the main melody, and it didn't seem at all ridiculous to Patrick. It sounded appropriate, as he returned to the present: clearing his mind, leaping to a standing position, holding his gun. He tested his shoulder with a finger. It hurt like hell, but the bullet had passed clean through; he was still alive, and he still had use of his arm.

Belatedly he realized the extent of the turmoil around him. The main door was about to give, shuddering with each blow struck by the police battering ram. Patrick looked to Robert but he was already moving, pulling two tear gas canisters from the bag. Sandro had left the control box and was rushing forward, screaming in fury. Patrick moved toward him, waving his hand.

He said, "Sandro, no. I'm okay, I'm not hurt..."

It was too late: Sandro's friend was shot and he was angry now. He fired a low burst from a machine pistol as the SWAT team finally forced the door, charging into the room, yelling orders and wild exhortations, forcing the gang of three to retreat. Robert hurled the tear gas at the door and smoke billowed out in thick, bright-white clouds. The three of them made for the fire exit, Patrick shouting above the din, "Aim for their legs!"

They snapped the lock and stumbled out into a corridor as the cacophony of guns and voices and heavy boots rose. And Patrick had a moment of exquisite clarity then, everything around him reduced to its essence. This must be what war is like, he thought: chaotic, terrifying, thrilling, *insane*. And unreal. The whole thing felt surreal, like another movie scene, but a different one this time, something otherworldly and unnerving and beautiful. Time slowed down to dreaminess, then speeded up to a frightening velocity, as pieces of masonry chipped off under gunfire, ricochets resounded, and urgent commands were issued by the SWAT team leader.

The gang broke through a door and into another corridor. Robert and Sandro sprinted ahead and Patrick followed, and halfway down a middle-age cleaning woman, who'd somehow been left behind, emerged from a door. He almost bumped into her; he stopped; she looked at him, curious but oddly unafraid. Then he took her in his arms and waltzed her to the music playing in his head, spinning twice, three times, smiling at her from beneath his mask, before hurling her back into the room and running off. She peeked out from behind the door as gunsmoke and noise, paint and concrete sparking off the walls, heralded the arrival of the SWAT team moments later.

Up ahead they ran along another corridor, all looking horribly alike in the current straits. Patrick stopped at an emergency door. He called to them, pointing at it. "Hey! Hey, you guys!"

Robert and Sandro stopped and turned, and Patrick said, "It's used by maintenance and cleaning staff. Come on—over here."

He pushed the bar and the door opened into a circular stairwell. Sandro stood to shoot a few covering rounds but came under fire. He dived to the floor, covering his head. The police were gathering behind a corner now, firing off quick bursts in two-man relays, then ducking behind the concrete again. Robert and Patrick rushed back, Patrick shooting, not really aiming. Just keep firing. Distract them. Scare them. Buy some time.

Robert crouched beside him, rummaging in his bag for another canister of tear gas. As he stood to throw, a bullet clipped the top of his forehead. Just skimmed the skull, it seemed, sizzling through the bone. Robert didn't even cry out—he spun elegantly and dropped down dead. Patrick froze, letting his gun clatter to the floor then screaming in grief: "Jesus! *No*! Robert…"

Sandro grabbed Patrick and shoved him toward the door, shouting, "He's *gone*, Paddy! Just keep moving. Robert's gone. Don't think about it, just keep fucking moving…"

He pushed both of them through the door and Patrick down the stairs, and jammed the door behind them with a rifle. And then they were running, hurtling down the clanging metal steps, as the sounds of battle faded into the distance, and the Percy Faith waltz playing in Patrick's head faded out, too, whirling, whirling, like seabirds turning in the wind, tiny black specks spinning across an azure summer sky…

End of year round-up 2005
"Farewell to.." **Patrick Brode**

Age: 18
Nickname: none, really. 'Paddy' to my family
Hair: blonde/fair
Eyes: blue
Height: six foot and a tiny bit more
Girlfriend: still with the lovely Lillian (hope she mentions *me* in her questionnaire)
Clubs and societies: edited *Saints Alive!* for one year; computer club; played a little soccer; karate club
Favorite food: anything made from entirely artificial ingredients
Favorite drink: coke in crushed ice
Favorite TV show: none. It's the drug of the nation, haven't you heard?
Favorite movie: I suppose *The Godfather* movies. And one of the *Ernest* series for laughs
Favorite book: *The Handmaid's Tale* by Margaret Atwood
Favorite album: still *Nevermind*, probably
Favorite sex symbol: female – ooh, lemme see…maybe Kim Novak in her prime; male – that Croatian guy on *ER*. (You wanted both, right?)
Favorite place: inside my head (man)
Favorite item of clothing: ironic t-shirts in bright colors
Best memory of school: kissing four different girls at the Hallowe'en dance two years ago. I was young and stupid back then!
Worst memory of school: see above
Where are you going now: all the way to Killafornia, baby, to study English literature
Ultimate ambition: to live my life as a new paradigm!

We say: 'Most likely to marry a supermodel!'

Chapter 11

The value of a proper ending

AN EDDY of cream in a cup of coffee. Patrick looked at its off-white tail as it slowly revolved, turning his coffee a lighter brown. He and Sandro sat at a low table, on the couch, in the sitting room of a crummy apartment in Brooklyn Heights. The place belonged to Sandro's second cousin; he was on the road a lot, touring, doing the lighting for a blues-rock band.

Light sneaked in through the half-drawn curtains and Patrick continued to stir his coffee. Sandro glanced over at him: Patrick looked wiped-out, in every conceivable way. A dull stain had appeared at the shoulder of his t-shirt, that brown-red, old-rust color of dried blood. Sandro watched him for a moment more, then gently took the spoon.

He said, "Hey…I think you've stirred it enough. Drink."

"I don't…feel much like drinking, Sandro."

"Alright. That's cool."

They sat without speaking for a long while, the hum of the refrigerator a low, insistent back-note. Sandro stood, peeked cautiously out the window and sat down again. Nothing happening outside. No squad cars squealing to a stop on the street below, no panicked officers with firearms drawn, furtively glancing upward, swallowing their fear, and committing themselves to doing what needed to be done. They were safe for now, Sandro reasoned. About 16 hours had passed since they escaped the television studio, discarding their masks, hurriedly changing into street clothes in a rank public toilet, dumping the bags and weapons, strolling to this apartment as casually as they could manage while their heads pounded and their hearts broke apart.

They hadn't had the will to check the news reports on television since then. Neither of them wanted to see it made real in the cold, bright, all-encompassing gaze of the camera. But at least they were safe here, for now.

Eventually Patrick stood up with a forced smile and said, "I'll put some music on. Might help to…you know, distract us or…"

"Okay, Paddy."

Patrick flicked on an old, battered stereo sitting on a shelf and scanned through the different stations. Snatches of music and voices, talk shows and jingles, chart countdowns and thumping beats. He eventually stopped as a gentle, piano-led tune began. Patrick knew this song: *Soon After Christmas* by Stina Nordenstam, a fragile, haunting, achingly beautiful piece. His shoulders began to shake and he gripped the shelf tightly.

Sandro stood up and spoke after a long pause: "Paddy…"

Patrick waved a hand at him to stay back. He steadied himself, then spoke in a quavering voice. "I'm…alright, Sandro. I'm alright. I'm just…you know."

"Yeah, man. I know."

The two of them sat side-by-side on the little couch. Patrick ran his hands through his hair and smiled at Sandro. He said, "So what now, amigo?"

"We'll think of something, Paddy. *You'll* think of something. Just give it a little time."

Patrick nodded and gazed into the middle distance, moved by his friend's support and respect, listening to the music, to Stina's little girl voice with its sublime profundity of sadness.

Danny moved through the wreckage in the Network 4 building, surveying the scene, listening to the voice on the other end of his cell phone. Jesus, what a mess. And there it is, Danny boy: what a godawful *mess*. The place had been shot up pretty badly, which didn't surprise Danny in the slightest: those SWAT guys, to his mind, were the frat boys of every police force. Young, gung-ho, and irredeemably stupid. Shoot first and take aim later. A forensics team picked through the debris, and Danny wondered why they were bothering: what could they reasonably hope to find among this accumulation of splinters, chunks of masonry, broken glass, spent shells, and one dead body? And besides, it was all academic: there wasn't any doubt about who they were after now. Broder was his man.

He listened impatiently for a few moments and then said, "I don't fucking *know*, James. This is an old building; there's all sorts of corridors and stairwells and crap that even the owners don't know about. The kid worked here, for Christ's sake. Probably knew this place like the back of his hand. ...What? Yes, I know it's not good enough, but there you have it. He got away from us, alright?" He stopped at a door and lit a cigarette; to hell with the law. "And can I just say, James, that if that bonehead SWAT team hadn't barged in there like a bunch of drunken militiamen, I wouldn't have lost sight of Broder in the first place. Did you know Cathy Morrissey fractured her collarbone in the fall...? Yeah, well, there's something to get pissed about. Yeah, I know it wasn't your fault... Hold on, I've another call coming through..."

Danny pressed the call change button and stepped through a door, over a small pile of rubble, into a corridor. He started walking and said, "Yeah, go ahead... Peter. I didn't expect... Uh-huh... No, it's fine. I'm fine. I wasn't...really involved, I was too far back. Uh-huh... Listen, Peter, I gotta go. I've got the Captain on the other line. I'll call you tomorrow, okay? ...I promise, I promise. Take care." He switched lines again. "James, yes... Look, can we just stop fighting about this, please? Neither of us was to blame. And this isn't over yet. Patrick is still out there somewhere. ...No, I'm *not* 'calling him Patrick now.' I just said it, it doesn't mean anything. I barely met the kid for five minutes. Anyway, forget that—what was the damage to our guys? ...Uh-huh. No fatalities. That's good, that's good to know..."

He crushed the cigarette underfoot and walked through another door into one of the Network 4 canteens, a sterile, washed-out place, much the same as every other corporate canteen he'd ever been in. Cathy sat at the far side, by a window, nursing a coffee. Her right side was strapped up in a sling. She waved at Danny with her left hand; he waved back and held up a finger.

"Alright...alright... I gotta run, James. I'll call you later when

I know more, okay? ...Talk to you then."

He filled up a Styrofoam cup at the self-serve counter and carried it over to Cathy, sitting opposite her. She smiled sadly. Danny pointed to her collarbone.

"How's the injury?"

Cathy shrugged. "Aw...it's alright. I'll live."

"Okay. Good."

They sat in silence for a long moment. Then Cathy leaned forward and said, "Danny, I..."

"Hold on. Please. There are a few questions I have to...things that I want to know. About Patrick."

"Shoot." She smiled. "Sorry. No pun intended."

Danny smiled also. "I think I know the answer to this one already, but...did you ever suspect, Cathy? Anything?"

Cathy shook her head. "No. Nothing. He was just...Patrick, you know? A guy I worked with."

Danny said, "Well, I mean...what kind of guy did he seem to you? Honestly."

"He seemed...nice. He *was* nice. I never found him anything but sweet, and smart, and funny, and yahda yahda yahda. He was a nice kid. Honestly."

Danny leaned back and breathed out slowly.

"So...is there anything you've found out?" Cathy asked. "About what started all of this?"

He shook his head. "Nah. I mean, we know some of the background details a little better now. Robert—the guy you met, the guy who was here last night? His full name was Robert Eustace. Grew up in LA. Patrick and he met in university, they took a lot of courses together, played sports, traveled South America, Europe... Best friends, I guess." Danny paused. "He, uh...he had a son."

"Patrick?"

"No, Robert. He had a son, a two-year-old. With a former girlfriend. She received a package this morning—couriered with no return address."

Cathy raised an eyebrow.

"Don't worry, it was nothing…weird," Danny said. "It was actually a set of his old college books. You know, novels, poetry, literary criticism, that sort of thing."

"Right. And the third member? The big guy?"

"Believed to be—we're not 100 per cent sure yet—Alessandro Tomassi, a childhood friend of Patrick. His oldest friend, I suppose. Alessandro's been a roadie, a sound engineer, a mechanic…he's done different things. We talked to his mother earlier today. She hasn't seen him since he left home at about 17, so…we can't be definite that it's him. Yet."

Cathy looked away and said softly, "Alessandro. Nice name."

"Yeah, it is. A sonorous Italian name. Alessandro."

They smiled at each other and lapsed into silence again. Eventually Cathy put her hand on Danny's arm. She said, "Listen. You've got work to do, you've got things to check out. Go on. Don't let me hold you up."

"Yeah. I suppose I should really… Are you sure you'll be okay?"

She nodded vigorously and pointed into the distance. "Positive. Go. Get out of here."

"Okay." Danny stood up. "Listen, Cathy—would you like to meet for a drink some night this week? Just to…you know. Talk things through. I don't know why, but this whole thing has gotten to me on a really personal level, you know?"

She smiled and shook his hand. "I'm not surprised. That'd be great, Danny. Thanks."

"And don't worry, I won't make a pass at you or anything. I, ah—what's the phrase? 'Bat for the other side.'"

"I figured."

Danny smiled. "Okay, then. I'll call you?"

She nodded yes; Danny tipped her a salute with his finger and moved to leave, then stopped and turned back. He said, "You know the really funny thing? I sort of half-agree with what the stupid bastard was aiming to do—but I still have to take him down. It was wrong."

"I know you do," Cathy said. "And I think Patrick knows that, too."

The sun was slowly setting, shadows lengthening and the world bathed in that lovely amber glow, as Sandro and Patrick clasped hands and embraced on the street outside an adult bookstore and a small premises dealing in used car parts. A dour-faced Asian man selling hot food from a stall looked at them for a second, then went back to his work. Sandro hoisted a huge rucksack onto his back.

Patrick took a step back and appraised him, like a fretful mother sending her child to school for the first day, and said, "So you'll be okay? What time are you meeting this guy?"

"About 8.30. Don't worry: Raul is cool. He takes an alternative route out of the country. He'll get us there."

"Alright. Good. Don't get fucking caught now, okay?" He laughed nervously.

"I won't," Sandro said. "I'm gonna wait in that bar across the street. No cops in there."

"Right. Well. I guess I'd better go. A few things to do."

Sandro nodded. They embraced again.

"E-mail a contact number to my hotmail address in about a month," Patrick said. "You know the one. I'll call you from wherever I am."

"You got it."

Patrick swallowed dryly and said, "Take care, big guy."

"You too, Paddy."

Patrick took a few steps away before turning back. Sandro hadn't moved.

"Hey. You did the right thing," Patrick called. "Last night. You did the right thing in leaving Rob like that. It's what he would have wanted us to do."

Sandro nodded again. "You did the right thing too, man. All of it. It was the right fucking thing. Don't forget it."

Patrick nodded this time. Then he turned on his heel and started walking away.

A deep breath; insert the coin and dial. "Detective Danny Everard, please. Okay… No, his voicemail is fine." Patrick waited for a moment, looking around edgily. "It's me. Midnight; the roof of the old warehouse in Brooklyn. You know where I mean. And Danny—please come alone."

Danny didn't bother telling anyone else about the call. This wasn't something to divulge to someone else, opening it up to communal analysis, a rational appraisal. There was nothing rational about this whole case, he smiled to himself, so why change now? And more than that, he knew: this was one of those rare moments in life, when the moment itself takes on volition, a momentum uninfluenced by those involved. It was as if you stepped into the moment and became a part of it.

He pushed hard and the roof doors swung open, banging loudly on the concrete outside, and Danny thought: Aw, shut up, Everard. "Stepping into the moment." What kind of horseshit is that? He chambered his gun, replaced it in its holster, and flipped open the clasp. He walked through the doors—unlocked, as he'd known they would be—and out into a high breeze. Danny stumbled, surprised by the strength of the wind, and regained his balance. He took a deep breath, ran a hand through his hair, and stepped into the moment anyway.

He stood, in the center of the roof, waiting; eyes closed, fingers tensed, and ready to move for the gun. He didn't hear Patrick behind him until the younger man spoke.

"I knew you'd come alone. That you'd do that much for me."

Danny turned, slowly, until he was facing Patrick; he made a slight bow of acknowledgement, as if to say: You're welcome. Patrick was dressed in jeans and a t-shirt, with a picture of some big-haired heavy metal band on the front. Irony as a force in the world; Danny could appreciate that. Patrick wasn't wearing a balaclava, and he looked much younger, more boyish than Danny remembered, hair blowing around his eyes in the glow of the streetlights.

"And I knew you were gay," Patrick said. "From the first moment I met you. I suppose I have a feel for these things. That's why I foolishly thought you'd understand what we were trying to do."

"I did understand. I understood completely. But it was *wrong*, Patrick. It was wrong, and I'm duty-bound to stop it."

"I know you are. I understand you, too."

Danny nodded to himself, thinking, realizing. "You wanted me to know it was you. At the studio, with the phone in the wastepaper basket. Messing around like that, taking risks. You wanted me to know, didn't you?"

Patrick shrugged and didn't speak for a long while. Eventually he said softly, "Sometimes…some of our actions can take on a life of their own. Don't you think so? They go beyond our control."

He started lazily scratching one arm. He looked so callow, so guileless, standing there, hip cocked in a vaguely feminine pose, that it was almost infuriating.

"Patrick, come on," Danny said. "You know what I have to do here."

"I won't let you send me to jail, Danny. I couldn't face that."

"Hey, I don't have a choice. This isn't driving without insurance or casual fucking drug use—two people are dead." Danny stopped. "Your *friend* is dead."

Patrick smiled, his eyes faraway, his fingers lightly rubbing the goose bumps on his arm. He didn't move to speak. Danny shook his head angrily, then spread his arms wide.

"A stand-off on the rooftop? A bit clichéd for you, isn't it?"

"Yeah, sure it's predictable..." Patrick shrugged. "Can't be Oscar Wilde all the time, you know?"

Silence hung between them. The wind off the East River whipped about their heads and for some reason Danny noticed that an advertizing banner had come loose from a partially constructed building nearby. He couldn't make out the words, it was being buffeted about too quickly.

He took a step forward and said, "For God's sake... This has gone too far, okay? You can end it right now."

Patrick smiled. "Or you can, Danny."

He pulled his balaclava from his back pocket and began fitting it on his head.

"What are you...? Don't. Listen to me," Danny said. "I know what you're trying to do here. Think about what you're doing."

Patrick spoke through the wool, his words slightly muffled: "I am. I have done. I always do. That's sort of the point."

Danny swallowed hard and said, "Patrick, *please*—drop the gun. Please. You won't win, kid. You won't beat me."

Light glinted from the barrel of the pistol Patrick had pulled from his waistband. He smiled at Danny, teeth visible in the mouthpiece of the balaclava.

"You seem an educated, cultured man; let me recite a few words from a song. 'Leave the road and memorize this life that passed before my eyes...nothing is going my way.' What do you think, Danny? Did we make our statement?"

Danny looked away, looked down. He smiled wryly and nodded, as if in agreement. He flexed the fingers of his right hand. He smiled and raised his eyebrows and said, "Every writer knows the value of a proper ending. So long, Mr. Wilde."

Their eyes locked for a split-second, then both men moved. In one motion Danny dived to the side, whipped his gun out, and fired twice. It cracked into the night air, it echoed across the darkness.

Roundfire Books, put simply, publish great stories. Whether it's literary or popular, a gentle tale or a pulsating thriller, the connecting theme in all Roundfire fiction titles is that once you pick them up you won't want to put them down.